The Insanity Cookbook

The Insanity Cookbook

LIFE THROUGH THE DREAMSCAPE

Authored by
Jennifer Parker

Supplement by
John Allen Parker

These are works of fiction. Names, characters, places, and incidents are either the product of the author's imagination or are used fictitiously, and any resemblance to actual persons, living or dead, business establishments, events, or locales is entirely coincidental.

Copyright © 2013 Jennifer Parker
All rights reserved.

ISBN: 1492109312
ISBN 13: 9781492109310

AUTHOR'S NOTE

I have always suffered from a bizarre combination of insomnia and vivid dreams; dreams *so* vivid that sometimes I think they are real and operate on mistaken perceptions for days. Combined with the insomnia, the perceptions can become a little obsessive. When this happens I feel like I'm just a bit crazy. Occasionally my dreams are so weird that I know them immediately to be dreams – and yet, they still occupy my thoughts. It is the *weird* that inspired *The Insanity Cookbook*. The recipes that stand as road signs between segments of this book are made up of those dreams and should not be tried at home, i.e. I do not actually recommend cooking with kitty litter!

ACKNOWLEDGEMENTS

Editor: Ian Cole
Cover Art: Stephen D. Parker, Summit Graphic Design
Photography by Justin Dernier, Points North Photography

TABLE OF CONTENTS

CAT LITTER CASSEROLE

Grease 8 X 8 Pan and Preheat oven to 350 degrees

Ingredients:
1 Cup Melted Butter
½ Cup Bread Crumbs
1 Egg Lightly Beaten
½ Teaspoon Salt
½ Teaspoon Pepper

Cube fresh chicken breasts, soak in milk, and coat with mixture.

Roll individual chicken pieces in Cat Litter and layer in greased pan.

Bake 25 minutes.

I remove the finished casserole and marvel at its delectable aroma and appearance. Suddenly a horrible thought rushes through my mind and I drop the hot Pyrex to the floor where it shatters and the steaming dish—glass and all—vanishes. The thought: I can't possibly make this dish. I don't have a cat!

Short Stories

Some recommended for mature audiences, some—not for the feint of heart, and all—for those with open minds and open hearts for the human experience in all the seasons of life.

TRAINING

"One, two, three"—and we jumped. Adrenaline pumped, pulses raced, we hit the metal rungs simultaneously and the rumble of the train shimmied up from my feet to the hair on my head.

We couldn't hear each other over the roar of the great iron wheels rumbling down the track and the occasional piercing cry of the whistle, so we'd long since given up trying, but Liz gave me a grinning thumbs up. I hung back from the racing boxcar as far as my curled fingers and toes would allow, giving the wind free reign of my hot cheeks.

I was thirteen and a half. Liz had just turned. We'd been doing this two or three times a month in good weather since we were eleven. A few other kids had tried it. Luther Watts had made it once but he fell backwards and scared the hell out of everybody. Then Liz and I continued to do it alone.

Liz moved to Checawe when we were in second grade. She lived on the wrong side of the tracks. That's what my mom said. I never really understood what made one side right and one side wrong, but it was true that she lived on the *other* side from me, and once we got past that first winter when she tried to steal my ice skates by writing her name over mine in permanent marker, we were friends. Sort of. I didn't know why my mom didn't like her, and the wind blew just as coldly on me at her house.

—⋙—

I was fascinated by trains; always had been. When I was six my sister, Margaret, and her friend Julie let me walk with them across the trestle when there was only a single track and the thrill of the risk enticed me even then. Later, I would sit alone on the bank at the edge of town where the north and southbound tracks met and just watch.

The conductor would blow the whistle and wave whenever he saw me. The rumble warmed my body and the whistle always sounded lonely and beckoning, like I belonged somewhere else and didn't know why.

Liz felt it too. Or she *said* she did. I loved the trains. I think that she just liked taking risks. The first time I did it, she dared me to jump as the boxcars passed.

"Just jump," she said. "Just jump up and grab the ladder on the side and see how long you can hang on."

When I hesitated, she added, "What's the matter? You chicken?"

One thing I was not, even at eleven, or ever, was a chicken. And I've always been a sucker for a dare. So I took off—barefoot, running alongside the lumbering train, gravel scraping my summer-calloused soles. I could feel the train's rhythm in my heartbeat. I could smell oil and steam and freshly mown grass, and for just a moment I worried that the ladder rungs might be slippery. Then I was airborne. My right hand closed over the third rung and I swung myself up, curled the toes of both feet around the lowest rung, and then reached higher with my left. It was just that simple and I was climbing toward the top. I looked back and saw Liz, hands on hips, slack-jawed stupid, standing in my dust—and I shouted for joy. Face to the wind, I stretched back to feel the full extent of the freedom of flying my own boxcar. "See how long you can hang on," she'd said. Are you kidding?! I could hang on forever! But I didn't know where the train was going, so I jumped, making sure to clear the tracks by a good margin and rolled in the dirt. Then I lay flat on my back and stared up at the hazy sun, feeling like I'd just conquered the world.

I heard her feet kicking up the gravel and her lungs on overtime, but I didn't look back. She called out but I ignored her, closing my eyes and absorbing the vibrations of the fast disappearing train in the muscles of my legs and back.

"Are you okay? Did you fall?" She actually sounded concerned.

I laughed and finally looked at her. "So…you chicken, or what?"

"God! You scared me." She fell prone beside me. "So, how was it? Were you freaked or what?

"It was awesome. It was the coolest thing I ever did in my life." I couldn't help laughing and stretching my arms toward the sky. "I'd have stayed on if I'd known where I could jump and take the southbound back."

"That's easy," Liz said. "You could take this seven miles to the Summit underpass, hang out for about half an hour and take the southbound back. It would be so quick, no one would even miss us."

"Us?"

"Us. Tomorrow. Here. 3:30."

—⚏—

That was how it started. The 3:30 northbound, just out of sight of the depot. Seven miles of wind in our faces, half an hour of reading the Summit underpass graffiti, then south with the sun warm on our backs. All that summer we rode for free; for freedom.

Oh, there were moments. I took one pretty good fall, spent a couple of weeks with very little skin left on my arms, legs, and the left side of my face...told my folks I'd wiped out on my bike. They bought it, fussed a little. No big deal. Liz missed a few times (lacking in dexterity, in my opinion) and I either made the trip alone or jumped. When I left her behind on the gravel bank I got confused. First I'd feel superior, then bored, then guilty. The next summer she didn't miss as often and whenever she *did* I didn't go on without her.

It's funny, but we never talked very much. We didn't need to. We both loved the trains, the risk, the rush. We loved the wind in our faces, the feeling of flying. We could spend hours lying on the ground staring up at the sky and not saying a word. Liz came to my house a few times and my mother was polite to her, the way she was to the cleaning lady or to my guitar teacher, because he had long hair and smelled like marijuana. At least that's what I heard her tell my father when she thought I wasn't listening. Liz didn't seem to notice the politeness, but I noticed when I went to her house that her mother was very *impolite* to me, and somehow it felt exactly the same as my mother *being* polite, so I got the message. I was twelve, not stupid.

At the Summit underpass, we discovered a loose brick that could be worked all the way out with a little twist and pull. The gap made an ideal hiding place and Liz and I had our first serious discussion. What should we conceal there? Liz's mom smoked Kools and she figured she could pilfer a pack without getting caught. I got a couple of books of matches from the café where my sister was a waitress and we added a pack of Dentyne (just in case anyone decided to smell our breath), and a red felt marker for making political statements. It just seemed right to add this new dimension to our rebellion, and we took turns attempting to blow smoke rings—unsuccessfully—and adding to the Summit underpass graffiti.

There was snow in the air on our last trip before I turned thirteen and we made a pact to come back together on the first nice Saturday in the spring. To seal the deal, we restocked our hidey-hole with a fresh pack of Kools, gum, and matches. We put our initials and the date on the brick with a new green marker, added it to the cache, and then pushed the brick neatly back into place.

—⟋⟍—

It was the spring when we were thirteen that a few other kids tried it. Liz had been bragging. It felt wrong somehow, like no one else should do it. If she took other people to the Summit underpass, would she also show them our hiding place? I couldn't help but wonder. We still didn't talk much, so I didn't ask her. Then Luther fell and everyone just kind of left us to it. I didn't care. I just loved the trains, the wind, the underpass, even the sunburn and mosquito bites. I didn't even care about the stolen cigarettes anymore. Liz smoked them alone, quiet, trying her hand at creative profanity with a bright blue marker.

It was a hot, humid summer day, when July is unforgiving and even a soft landing jump makes your sunburn sing. I rode alone when Liz didn't show. I lay on my back in a Summit Township field near the underpass and chewed on a blade of grass; tempted a garter snake to curl up around my wrist; admired the clouds. I didn't like the underpass anymore. It was smoky and dirty, and the graffiti had gotten stupid. I wondered where Liz was and then realized that I wasn't really sure I cared. I rode the trains for myself. But I rode because she'd dared me in the first place…and it was still the coolest thing I'd ever done.

I heard the whistle and raced back across the tracks to grab the southbound train home. A creeping doubt was nagging at me and drove me from the train straight to Liz's door. I was going to have it out with her. Were we friends or not?

—◆—

She was sitting on the steps of the sagging front porch. When she saw me she got up and darted inside. The sound of a flat handed slap and a shrieked oath sent her scuttling out again backwards.

"Hey," I said, uncertain now that I was there just exactly *why I was* there and what I'd even come to say.

"Hey," she answered without turning.

The porch door flew open so hard that the lower hinge popped and the wood cracked. Liz's mother shoved her so that she fell back down the steps to the weedy, littered yard. I moved just fast enough to grab her shoulders and pillow her head before she hit the ground.

"You stupid little bitch!" the woman screamed at me. "Get out of my yard before I call the cops!"

I looked down at Liz's battered face. Her left eye was swollen bigger than my whole fist, her lip split in two places, and there were bruises from her hairline to chin. I couldn't speak.

"You want to kill yourself, you go head, girlie! But you leave my goddamn daughter alone, do you hear me?"

I could feel Liz quaking but I still couldn't move; couldn't speak.

"Are you deaf or just stupid?" she screamed. "Get off my property now!"

"Liz?" I said quietly. There were red spidery veins running through the white of her right eye.

"Just get the hell out of here," she ordered as she pulled herself up. Her t-shirt hiked up in the back and I could see striped bruises across her tailbone.

I don't remember getting up or turning away. I don't remember running, but I was suddenly running with all my strength—straight to the tracks. It was nearly sunset and there was a train going south. I grabbed a rung, swung myself up, and held on. I leaned back as far as I could and let the wind dry my face. This was *my* ride! Only this time, I had no idea where I would jump.

FOR SALE

"Do you mind if I look inside?"

Elsa paused and looked around for the source of the question, but there was no one there.

The wind, she chastised herself, *just the wind.*

She shook her head and returned to her raking. It was only half done and damn, if it didn't feel like snow. Elsa could feel it in every one of her arthritic joints. Why the hell was she out here raking anyway? She could hire some young kid to do it. God knew she could afford it. Hank's insurance money would pay for it.

A slight muscle spasm caught at her back and she paused again. That was happening more and more lately. She just couldn't convince her old body to slow down and take it easy. She guessed she was just like Hank in that way. He'd never taken it easy either.

"Do you mind if I look inside?"

She stiffened when she heard the voice again, and turned around. She was startled to see a young woman standing where no one had been only moments ago. Elsa took a bandana from her apron pocket and swabbed her forehead to cover her momentary perusal of the girl in front of her.

Obviously one of those Yippies, Elsa thought as she eyed the sleek silk suit and faultless makeup. The suit was tailored, much like the one Elsa herself had worn on her wedding day, but *she* would never wear so much paint on her face.

"Excuse me?" Elsa looked toward the driveway and the gravel road beyond. No car. She frowned.

"I saw the sign. I'd like to see inside."

"Look, I'm just trying to sell the place. I'm no real estate agent. If you want to see the house you have to make an appointment with her."

"Oh." The girl lowered her eyes and bit her lower lip, somehow managing not to damage her flawless gloss job.

"Look," Elsa fished in her apron pocket through tattered tissues, hairpins, and cough drops, finally coming up with what she wanted. "Here's her card. You can call her. Century 21. In town." She pointed, hoping to draw the girl's attention away from her home.

"It's a lovely house. I'd just like to see the inside for a moment."

"Don't know what a young girl like you would want with a broken down old house like this." Elsa said. "Not that there's anything really *wrong* with it. It just doesn't seem to me to be the kind of place that you'd like. There's not even a shower."

"Please?" the girl entreated. "I want to see inside. I won't take long, I promise. It's very important to me."

"Can't you just call the agent? I have her number right here."

"Please," the girl said again. "I'm just passing through town and I don't plan on returning after today." She reached out a slender, expensively manicured hand and touched Elsa's withered, blue-veined one. Her voice had taken on a note of desperation that both irritated and touched the older woman. "I have to see it. Just once."

—⚶—

Elsa silently followed the girl from room to room, watching her eyes wander the walls, windows, and woodwork with undisguised emotion. Occasionally the girl touched something; a doorknob, or a window ledge. Her attention was everywhere at once, and Elsa could barely keep up with her. All she could do was look at the rooms that she'd inhabited daily for more than five decades. It was just a decrepit old house; at least that's how she'd come to think of it since Hank died. The woodwork was real pine, and she remembered how it reflected the light from the cut glass chandelier when she'd been young enough to worry about polishing woodwork and washing chandeliers. The floor was in worse shape than the woodwork, yet it too had once been beautiful—and could be again if Elsa cared about having it refinished.

The girl walked up the curved staircase, her hand caressing the wooden banister and spooled railing as she walked. Elsa followed, but when she ran her hand along the railing dust motes rose in the air. She looked critically at the dust left on her hand. When she was younger she'd have apologized for it. When she was younger she worried about what others thought. But that time was long gone.

In the bedroom, the girl touched the quilted comforter with the tips of her fingers. Elsa bit back the sharp words that sprang to her mind watching the girl. *No one* touched Hank's bed. She hadn't touched it herself in the last three months, choosing instead to sleep on the sofa. It was easier than facing his empty side of the bed night after night. A part of her wanted to throw this kid out, but she reminded Elsa of someone, someone who had touched the same bed in the same timid way so many, many years ago.

Where did she come from? What in the world brought her here to this house? She was undeniably too young to have ever lived in the house. She couldn't be older than twenty-eight or nine, and Elsa had moved into the house fifty-one years and two months ago; the day she became Hank's wife. The girl acted as if she had memories of this place, yet Elsa knew that it was impossible. She, herself, was assaulted by memories at every turn; it was why the brown and yellow sign now stood sentinel in the front yard. But what reason could there be for this whippersnapper's fascination?

Descending the staircase, the girl stopped to gaze at the sepia photograph that was the single adorning feature on the otherwise bare wall. She didn't say a word, but paused only for a moment and then drifted down the remaining steps. Elsa stopped too. She looked with dull blue-gray eyes into the same eyes; eyes that had been a deeper shade of blue then; translucent and radiating happiness. Her suit was tight, her hair upswept, and beside her stood Hank, the way he had looked in 1962, the way he often still looked in her dreams. Deep lines gathered between her eyes. The photograph was hanging crooked in its dusty frame. She didn't straighten it, but sniffed at the dust and continued down the stairs behind the girl who was boldly walking toward the back of the house.

They entered the kitchen with its chipped enamel sink and faded linoleum that Hank had always meant to replace. The refrigerator emitted a caustic buzzing that went unacknowledged. Elsa was too used to it to notice and the girl stood still with her eyes closed. Was she listening to it?

The kitchen was the last room and the tour of the house had taken less than ten minutes; ten minutes during which neither of them had spoken. Elsa was anxious for the girl to leave so she could return to her raking.

"The swing," the girl whispered.

"What?"

"The swing," she repeated, gazing out the kitchen window into the backyard where a wooden swing hung from a sturdy oak branch. Without asking, she drifted out the back door into the small yard, blanketed with autumn leaves, and made her way toward the porch-style swing gently swaying in the October breeze.

She knelt on the ground in front of the swing and placed her cheek against the wood. The gesture brought Elsa up short, wondering whether or not to intrude. She avoided the backyard these days, for the swing only reminded her of what could never be again. Funny. It was the swing that had drawn her and Hank to the house in the first place. It was on the swing where Hank had placed his hand on her belly and felt their baby move for the first time. It was on the swing where she and Hank had read their son's letters: from college in the 80s, from Kuwait and Iraq in the 90s. It was on the swing where they had held each other after the Marine chaplain had finally left them alone to grieve.

The girl rose and sat on the swing gently, her face serene, as if she'd come home after a long, long absence. She patted the seat beside her, looking up at Elsa.

Good Lord, Elsa thought. *Does she expect me to sit there beside her? Some stranger on our swing?* But she did so anyway, hesitantly. The silence was heavy for moments, until Elsa felt the girl's warm, soft hand again cover her own, and she hazarded a glance. The girl's pretty blue eyes were bright with tears, and as Elsa watched, they spilled over her lashes and made attractive wet trails down her cheeks.

"Thank you," the girl said softly, "thank you so much." She squeezed Elsa's fingers once and then stood and walked briskly toward the corner of the house.

"Wait!" Elsa called.

The girl stopped, turned, and waited.

Elsa felt suddenly bereft for no explainable reason. She wanted the pest to leave, didn't she?

She stood slowly, still clutching the cold chain of the swing in her left hand where the gold ring bit into her finger and glinted with the light of the setting sun.

"Good-bye," she called.

The girl smiled. Then she was gone

—m—

Elsa sat alone on the old swing. She felt tired and invigorated at the same time, she dozed a little, just swaying and thinking until the sun had set and the world was dark, barely noticing when the snow began to fall.

Some time later she ambled to the front yard to put the rake away. She wasn't really surprised to find the brown and yellow sign lying on its side near the lawn and leaf bag she'd been filling earlier. She took the time to stuff it into the bag with the dry leaves and twigs, tie the bag, and place it at the curb. She left it there with two identical, if slightly less awkwardly packed, bags.

Maybe tomorrow she'd do something about that woodwork. Maybe tonight she would sleep in her bed and hold Hank's pillow in her arms. Soft snow fell to the ground around her. She'd always loved the first snowfall. Now why had she forgotten that?

Elsa turned and walked into the house, turning off the yard light and closing the faded curtains. She walked past furniture that had seen better days and up a curved staircase with a dusty banister. She passed a crooked photograph and then returned to it. What a handsome man. Her fingers reached to straighten the picture and the lines around her eyes relaxed.

She continued on up the stairs to a room with a quilted comforter on a saggy bed with two pillows. She ran her fingers across one of them with the same tenderness that she had on her wedding night; the night she had made this her home. She turned down the bedding and held Hank's pillow tightly against her face. She thought she could still detect his vague scent and she drew strength from it. She turned off the bedside lamp and laid her head on her own pillow.

The woodwork, the chandelier, and a realtor to let go. Elsa smiled. Yes. She had a lot to do tomorrow.

PENNANT PENANCE

"Go girls! Bring it on home now!" He shouts beside me, thumping his big working man's hands together, painfully loud and close. I glance to my right, but he doesn't look at me. His eyes are on the field but a muscle is twitching in his jaw and I know he's thinking that I should be out there. *I'm* thinking that I should be out there.

"Thataway, Emily! Good slide!"

"One more!'

"No pitcher! No pitcher!"

Why can't I drown out their voices? Why can't I join them? What am I even doing here, sitting on these hard metal bleachers that are pinching my thighs? Why do I feel the sun burning my skin sitting here? I never even notice it when I'm out on the field?

I want to say, "I'm sorry, Daddy. Please forgive me." But I don't. I look down at the field. Coach is pacing along the first base line and he looks at the stands—right at me. Even from this far away I can see his jaw tighten and his eyes grow cold. I know that it isn't anger or hatred that I see. It's disappointment, which is so much worse. And I want to say, "I'm so sorry, Coach Molina. I'd take it back if I could. I'd do anything." But he looks back at the first pitch to the next batter and I don't say a word. I'm too far away anyhow, and it's been too long. I've waited too long.

The bat cracks and the high foul sails over the stands and into the parking lot behind us. All eyes turn my way. In my head I know that they're following the flight of the ball. But in my heart they're all staring at me. They're all thinking: *There she is. That's the girl who broke into the coach's office. There's the girl who blew her shot at a softball scholarship to St. Mary's her senior year.* Of course, most of them aren't really looking at me at all. Most of them don't even know me. We're 180 miles from home in the Section 6 final game. One more run and we're going to state. *They're* going to state, I correct myself. I'm not. Dad feels their eyes too, though. Beside me, I feel him stiffen.

—⅏—

All I had wanted was to have some fun. But I didn't want to tell the truth, so there we were. I didn't want to do it. Mr. Molina never did anything to me, but I was afraid that if I didn't go through with it, I would look like a crybaby geek in front of Jake. If Nikki hadn't asked me to say who I wanted to have kiss me right in front of him, I never would have taken the stupid dare. She knew I liked Jake, just like I knew my dad didn't like him, or Nikki, or Nikki's boyfriend, Eddie.

Eddie and Jake swore that the school alarm system only activated with movement in the hallways and common areas, and that the office windows weren't wired. I was so afraid that they were wrong. They hid down in the bushes and I was the one doing a Spiderman along the wall and window ledge. If I couldn't have fit through that little window Coach leaves cracked it would have been all over anyway. I hoped I wouldn't fit, but I did.

"Hurry up!" Nikki hissed at me from below.

"Shut up!" I whispered back. "I'm doing the best I can."

I heard them laughing down there. The sweat had my hands so slick that I couldn't get a decent grip on the inside of the window frame and my lip stung where I'd been scissoring it between my teeth, but I couldn't seem to let up on it.

There was enough light from the street lamps for me to see into the glass-fronted bookcase where he keeps his autographed baseball collection.

"Grab a good one." That's all they had said. I reached into the cabinet and closed my fingers around one at random. I squinted at it in the darkness. Mickey Mantle. "Damn good one," I whispered. I turned for the window but my elbow hit something on his cluttered desk and there was a crash. I froze for a second and then raced for the window. They weren't laughing anymore, I noticed.

I went down a heck of a lot quicker than I had gone up, I'll tell you that much, and we all ran like crazy back to Eddie's garage where we'd been playing truth or dare and sneaking cigarettes from the carton of Camels his dad kept hidden in his tool box.

Inside with the door shut and the fluorescents shining it all seemed pretty cool. Jake was impressed, I could tell. When I told them about it I pumped it up a bit, you know, kind of added to the drama a bit. The more I talked, the better it got, and Jake kept sitting closer and closer to me with his leg pressed tight against mine.

It was just a prank, I thought. Just a harmless little truth or dare. Jake noticed me, the cool kids accepted me, and I'd return the ball the next day. Oh yeah, I told myself all kinds of good lies. Only it wasn't harmless. And the *cool* kids turned on me, bragging around about the escapade and within a day I was busted. Coach and the school didn't charge me legally—but they suspended me for a week from school and for the rest of the season from the team. Coach didn't say a word. That's what hurt the most. He took the ball I handed to him and looked at it— never at me. He squeezed it and his face got tight, like he had sucked his lips right back into his face so that there was just this hard straight line. He nodded as Principal Jax handed down his ruling but he never said a word. He still hasn't. My dad sat there beside me—mirroring Coach's expression and nodding. During the week I sat at home I got the letter from St. Mary's—withdrawing their scholarship offer. No explanation. Just...*After reconsideration for admission and scholarships...* "

—◊—

The winning run is on third now. Emily. My best friend from fourth grade until stupidity. Gretchen, our second best batter at .371, is at the plate. It's the most exciting moment in our high school careers and

I'm seventy yards away from the plate; at least fifty from the mound—*my* mound; and out of uniform. Suddenly I can't draw a full breath and I hear a sound reminiscent of my dog begging for scraps. My eyes are burning and my blink reflex is on overdrive. His hand closes over mine and squeezes hard. I force my voice around the lump in my throat, "Daddy. Oh God, Daddy! I'm so sorry." As quickly as that his arms are around me in a bear hug like I haven't felt in years and he's stroking my hair and rocking me.

"Sshh…" is all I hear. "Sshh now, baby, sshh…"

I haven't seen him cry since my mom died four years ago, but he's crying now. Not making a scene or anything like I am. He's just holding me while I let it all out and people scoot a little farther away from us on the bleachers. He still loves me, I can feel it. I had wondered. Now I know. He'll love me if I go to State U or Community College, if I play softball or if I don't. I'm sick to my stomach but I'm feeling—feeling—*some*thing. I can do this, I think. My dad loves me. I can do this.

I hear the inimitable sound of a dead-on hit; aluminum on leather; feel the vibrations of a hundred people jumping to their feet on the metal bleachers, and hear the roar which tells me that Gretchen connected and Emily scored. I don't actually witness the win firsthand, but I feel it in every muscle of my body and I know what I have to do. He knows too, because he releases me, looks into my eyes, and nods. He turns back to the field and applauds with the rest, as I make my way toward the plate where my teammates are all gathered, celebrating, hugging, screaming.

My heart is pounding, the sound so loud in my ears that the cheering is distorted and unreal to me. I walk as if in a vacuum toward the circle that I am no longer a part of, and my eyes focus on Emily, praying that I'll see forgiveness in her eyes and that I can find the strength to finally apologize to Coach.

Some of the girls see me coming, I know. They nudge others who nudge others and I'm choking again, holding my breath. Emily and Gretchen are embracing in the middle of the huddle. I can tell when Gretchen notices me and says something I can't hear. Emily turns and her eyes lock on mine. I can't read her. I stop. She hesitates. The next thing I know she catapults into my arms and is hugging me and jumping and crying all at the same time. How can this feel so good and hurt so much all at once?

"You shoulda been here," she whispers in my ear.

"I know," I say. "God, Em. I miss you. I'm sorry. I'm so sorry."

"I know." She hugs me tighter.

I know she means it, I can feel it, and it's so damn humbling I can't believe it. I'm reeling in all of this already when I blink to clear my eyes and see him over her shoulder. Coach Molina. His expression makes me freeze. It's like the day I returned the baseball all over again. His expression is hard and unreadable. But I avoided looking into his eyes then and was too scared then to let him see that I was scared. I wouldn't break contact with him now.

Maroon and gray uniforms separate around us and Emily draws back, but keeps her arm around my waist protectively, still sniffling. The air around me seems charged with expectation and everyone is watching, waiting. I owe my whole team, and I know that. But I have one more real apology to make and this one is the hardest for me. How can I expect the man who'd made me a good enough ball player to deserve scholarship offers understand that I had stolen from him and violated his trust just to impress a guy who wasn't worth it a few hours later? How?

I'm still wondering, still looking into those gray somber eyes, when I see the thin line of his mouth relax, the gray glitters a little, and his shoulders drop as he opens his arms for me. *For me.* Willingly I step into his embrace and whisper my plea as the crowd erupts once more. Coach Molina presses his stat book into my stomach and says, "I'll be needing a manager at State. It's getting to be too much for the old man."

Then he turns and walks away toward the cheering crowd, and I look down at the book. Emily puts her arm around me again and several of my teammates pat my back or shoulder as they pass. I won't be playing, I know, and I haven't really redeemed myself. Not completely. But I look at Coach's back disappearing into the crowd and hold the book tightly to my gut and know that at least I'm on the right road.

SWEET DREAMS

"Why don't you go out on dates?"

"What are you talking about?"

"You know, dates. Why don't you?"

"Is dating the latest hot topic among eight year olds, or is this just personal concern for you old mom's social life?"

Mitchell giggles and gives me a gap-toothed smile before gobbling another forkful of macaroni and cheese. Personally I hope it's the end of the discussion. It's not.

"On T.V., grown up people always go out on dates."

"Oh they do, do they? I guess you and I must be watching different shows."

"It's true, Mom. They go to places for dinner and they dance and stuff. They get all dressed up, you know, Mom."

"Okay, Mitch," I say, deciding it's time to try a different tack. "I'll admit that in some shows there are people who date, but not on all shows and not all people. Besides, this is real life and not everyone dates."

His blue eyed glance drops to his plate where yellow cheese sauce has all but obscured the masked face of Batman, then focuses on me again.

"But why aren't *you* dating?"

"What's the sudden interest in my love life anyway? Why do you care if I'm dating or not, honey? Maybe you don't see it but I'm completely happy with my life just the way it is, and dating isn't all fun and games, Mr. Nosey. Relationships are full of problems and some of them can't be solved in thirty minutes like they are on television." I hear my own voice—louder and more annoyed than I intend—and I take a deep breath. I shouldn't be speaking to Mitchell like this.

"I'm sorry, Mitch." I reach across the tiny dinette table that I had rescued from an early demise at the county dump, and cover his small sticky hand with mine. "But you, of all people, should understand.

I know you're only eight, but you know things that a little boy shouldn't have to know…and you've seen things that a little boy shouldn't have to see."

Mitch looks like he's going to cry and I can't take it. Our crying days are past. I reach out to him and he leaves his place in favor of snuggling on my lap. He doesn't do that often these days. I stroke his blond head and kiss it softly. He smells of White Rain, cheese, and chalk—no man's cologne could ever be sweeter. The silence soothes and comforts as the light from outside fades from orange to purple to silver to black, and still we sit.

"Do you ever miss him?" he asks.

"No." I find that I am unable to lie to him. "No, Mitchell. I don't miss him. But if you do, it's okay you know."

For the first time since climbing onto my lap, he pulls away from my shoulder and looks directly into my eyes. I see telltale brightness, but he isn't crying. We don't cry.

His earnest voice trembles not in the least with his answer. "I hate him."

—m—

Dishes are done. Stories are read. Kisses are exchanged and prayers are said by the one of us who still believes. Soft light is filtering through the half open bedroom door, cutting the shadows across Mitchell's bed where I tuck the covers snugly around his chin.

"Mom?"

"What honey?"

"I love you."

"I love you too." I wait for him to go on, sensing that there is more. He just plays with the edge of his blanket, forming fuzzy fluff balls in his fingers. His forehead is wrinkled with concentration and he is biting his lower lip. Sweet quiet seconds pass.

"I just thought that maybe you would want to like somebody now."

"Now? I don't understand. What do you mean, *now*?"

"I mean that it would be good for you to like somebody now that he's really gone."

"Mitchell," I say, "he's been gone for more than two years."

"That's not what I mean, Mom."

I wait for him to go on but he doesn't. He's embarrassed for some reason. He seems younger suddenly, but his eyes appear infinitely aged and wise as he contemplates sharing his secret with me. Without taking my eyes from his, I sink to my knees beside his bed so he will know that I'm listening. "Honey, you can tell me. You can always tell me anything. What do you mean that he's gone?"

"He's gone from my dreams. I haven't had any nightmares about him for a long, long time. It's like he's really, finally gone. It's like I'm not afraid to come home from school anymore, or go to sleep anymore. I'm even starting to forget what he looked like, Mom. I'm starting to forget to always be scared and careful. You know, Mom?"

His voice has taken on a pleading quality, desperate for me to understand—to affirm his feelings, and to confirm his safety.

"You're absolutely right, honey. He is gone. He's gone from our lives and now he's gone from your dreams too. He can't hurt us anymore."

Funny…that lie wasn't so hard to say, I tell myself as I crawl between the icy sheets. Maybe Mitchell's nightmares are truly over now. If they are, I might just be grateful enough to regain some faith. But not likely.

As darkness closes around me I feel the accustomed struggle begin. It's a struggle to stay awake when my body and mind are exhausted. It's a struggle to escape the voice that's calling; the hands that are reaching. And for tonight, it's a struggle to own what my son has finally found—the right to sleep without dreams, and the peace that cannot exist with fear.

THE DRAGON SLIDE

"Guys!" The door to Mr. Schram's classroom opened with a bang as John raced in, his face ruddy from both cold and distress.

Peter, Dan, and Sherry turned toward the intrusion, while Schrambo pecked at his computer keys as if he didn't hear a thing—typical.

"They're tearing it down! Come on!"

"Slow down," Sherry ordered. "Who's tearing what down?"

Pete leaned in while Dan relaxed with his back against the white board, curious, but not quite ready to get emotional. After all, he was a senior and the others were just juniors. He had a rep to maintain.

John collapsed against a file cabinet, knocking Schram's phone off the hook. He was still puffing and held up a hand to quiet the others while he worked on getting his breath back.

"The dragon slide!" He finally said. "They're tearing it down."

That got Dan's attention. He rose to his full height and his eyes widened.

"No way! Who's tearing down the dragon slide?" asked Pete.

"The janitors. They're out there now. They've got it in pieces all over the place!"

"But why?" asked Sherry.

"I don't know. All that new crap I suppose. You know the drill—new age crap for new age kids who are too prissy to play on the old stuff." John's face reddened as his voice rose in anger.

"I can't believe my dad didn't tell me they were going to do something like that," Pete said. "He knows how much we love that thing! I mean, the school board would know something like that, right?"

"All I know is that they're tearing it down and..." John hesitated, lowering his voice with a glance toward the disinterested teacher across the room still pecking at the keyboard with the speed of a corpse. "I got my first kiss under that slide, guys."

"I got my last one," Sherry said quietly with a meaningful glance at Dan, who still hadn't said a word.

"Did you ask them what's going on? What they're going to do with it?" asked Pete.

"The dump!" John raged. "They said they're hauling it to the dump! Can you believe it?"

The others reacted with outrage that a piece of their childhood was going to be tossed like a hunk of garbage. The phone began making an irritating beeping noise. Schram-the-Man looked up and glanced around, looking for the source of the noise in a confused manner as if a fly were circling his head and then returned to his computer keys without a word. Dan rolled his eyes, rolled his shoulders, stepped forward, and said, "Let's go."

The four trooped out of the room and down a maze of hallways and staircases to the far end of the building that housed the elementary school. They could observe the demolition process through the windows without being observed. Sure enough, there it lay: the head of the dragon facing them, mouth open, serpentine tongue lolling out to the side. What had once looked ferocious now looked beaten and pathetic. Its entrails lay strewn behind; a string of curving metal remains.

Sherry pressed her forehead against the glass, "Oh God. It's dead."

"Not yet, it isn't," Dan said.

The others looked at him, it was obvious that he was formulating a plan, but they knew him well enough to wait and not press while he worked it out in his own head before bringing them in on it.

Finally he said, "Look, they're quitting for the day. It's cold. It's getting dark. They won't haul it off until morning at least, right?"

"Right," said John.

Sherry and Peter nodded.

"Can you get your dad's pickup?" he asked Pete.

"No problem."

"Good. Then everybody change into something dark, get some gloves, and meet on the north end of the playground at eleven o'clock." He put out his hand. John put his on top, then Sherry, then Peter. As their eyes met, John's face split into a wide grin as the others all nodded.

—◆—

They worked quickly and quietly in the cold autumn darkness, carrying the pieces of their mangled childhood to the bed of the truck, and just as quickly and quietly unloading them into the woods that backed both Dan and Sherry's houses. The righteousness of their mission insulated them from chills and fear of discovery and they all returned to their homes feeling slightly criminal—and slightly heroic.

—◆—

One by one, they were called from their classes the next morning. Sitting in the principal's conference room, not daring to make eye contact with each other, they faced off with not only the principal, Mr. Jacobs, but Looby, the town cop who generally couldn't find a lost dog or the turn signal on his squad car.

"A piece of equipment is apparently missing from the elementary school," Mr. Jacob's began. "I have it on good authority that the four of you were seen hanging around near there last night."

The four kids looked appropriately blank and confused, shrugging as if this were all news to them.

"Larceny is serious business kids," said Looby. His "tough" voice was negated by the view of something green stuck between his front teeth. "If you have something to say, you'd better say it now. It'll go easier on you later if you just 'fess up."

No one said a word, and the silence was punctuated by the ticking of the conference room clock.

Jacobs tried again. "Think how this will look. Four honor students? A preacher's kid, a teacher's kid, a banker's kid, and the son of the school board president…thieves?" He opened his mouth to continue, but was interrupted by a knock on the door.

Eddie, the head custodian poked his head in. "It's not there, Mr. Jacobs. We looked where he said." He jabbed an accusatory finger in Looby's direction. "And there's not a piece of it anywhere. We searched the woods behind that development for half a mile either way. There ain't no sign of the thing."

Looby colored.

Jacobs cleared his throat, and then ordered, "You four get back to class."

—⁂—

Nerves were on edge through the day and still were when the four met for their usual 3:15 get-together in Schram's room.

"You guys got nothing better to do than hang around here every day?" Schram greeted them as they entered.

Shrugs were the only answers he got.

"Well, come on then," he said. "I've got something you can help me with. My back is killing me and I figure you owe me for using my room as your private social club every day."

Still nervous over their "larceny" and their tenuous grasp on freedom, the kids followed their teacher to the parking lot, where he unlocked his car and said, "Get your wheels and follow me."

"Where the heck is he taking us?" John asked as Dan's car followed Schram's down the highway. "What could be way out here?"

"Schrambo's a weird one," said Sherry, "he could be planning to use us as some sort of ritual sacrifice or something."

They pulled off the highway onto a long curving driveway. Sheltering trees arched above and a rustic log cabin came into view. When both vehicles stopped in front of the cabin, all four of the kids got out, still looking at each other with a mixture of concern and curiosity. They followed the silent Schrambo as he walked behind the cabin. There, the pieces of their beloved dragon slide lay neat and orderly and ready to be reassembled in the shelter of trees and lake shore—far from the eyes of uptight school and legal officials.

Dumfounded, they looked at their slightly odd, and usually distracted teacher, as he reached under the cabin steps and pulled out a huge toolbox then turned back to them.

"My last kiss was under that slide too," he said quietly with a sporting grin. "Now get to work."

JUST A GIRL

"Who's it from, your advisor again?" Lisa asked, hoping to delay Thomas's inevitable departure just a minute longer.

Thomas didn't answer, too engrossed in the text message to even glance up. Lisa felt her heart clutch again. It seemed like every second she lived these days was a battle to keep her emotions in check, to keep from clinging, to pretend to be supportive. No. That wasn't really fair. She *was* supportive of Thomas's decisions to go to the University of Minnesota's main campus in the beginning. She had been nearly as thrilled as he was when he'd been offered a baseball scholarship at the Big Ten school. It had always been his dream, and because she loved him and loved watching him play, it had been her dream for him as well. At first it had just been exciting and she'd put out of her mind thoughts of the 300 miles that would separate them during her last year of high school in the tiny northern town where they had both grown up. Now that it was time for him to step onto the streamlined Greyhound bus that would bear him away from her she was finding it much more difficult to be objective.

"Thomas?" she tried again.

"What?" He looked up. "Sorry. What did you say?" He seemed so distracted these days, not at all like he used to be.

"I just asked if the text was from your advisor again?"

"Oh," he seemed to hesitate. "No. It's from the R.A. in the dorm I'm assigned to. She's just sort of welcoming me to the U and telling me what kinds of things I can expect, all that, you know."

Lisa's radar locked on to the only word he had said that mattered: "She?"

Thomas just looked blankly at her as if he couldn't comprehend the question or problem being stated in the single syllable she'd uttered. Lisa struggled for the control to keep her voice even and her face calm. "I mean, I didn't think that the R.A. in a guys' dorm would be a *she*." Lisa attempted a teasing smile with a lump rising in her throat, already becoming used to the way he held back important details from her; details he'd have willingly shared without thought just a couple of months ago.

"Well, I suppose that would be weird if it was a guys' dorm," Thomas said. "But it's co-ed. Most of the dorms are. It's no big."

No big, Lisa thought, *no big shouldn't hurt this much.*

Thomas's parents came out of the depot then. His mom was carrying the perforated ticket which seemed obscenely large from Lisa's distorted point of view and as if it were made of gelatin seen through her blurry eyes. If she didn't say something before they reached Thomas's side, she may miss her opportunity forever. "Thomas," her voice cracked, and he looked up as if surprised to see her on the verge of tears.

"Hey, what's wrong?" he asked.

She nearly choked on a laugh that bubbled up from nowhere at his insensitivity. What had happened to the boy who had promised to love her forever? Where was the sweet, shy gentleman who opened doors and slipped the first spring lilacs through the vents of her locker just because he knew that they were her favorite and that she always bemoaned the fact that they didn't last long enough? Where was her first love, her first kiss, her only faith in mistletoe, valentines, and fireworks? She had to say something, but her only reply to his ill-chosen question with his parents closing in quickly was, "Nothing. Nothing."

He chucked her under the chin with his knuckles—like one of the guys—and smiled.

"All set honey?" his mom asked.

"Yup," he answered, suddenly king of the monosyllable.

"You've got all your paperwork? You remembered your wallet?" asked his dad.

"Everything's cool, Dad. No worries." Thomas answered with the same smile he'd just given to Lisa.

The driver honked and the last few people milling about headed for the bus steps and destinations unknown to Lisa. No one was looking at her. Suddenly she felt completely out of place. Thomas wasn't looking at her and his parents had eyes only for him. Suddenly she was just a girl.

Lisa had always been just a girl, but now she knew that she was more than that. Now she was just a girl he'd once known; just a girl back home.

THE BIRTHDAY

She jumped, hitting the alarm button with shaking fingers. The gripping pain struck her as it did every day at this time and her small hands clutched at her stomach for a moment, willing it away. She set the alarm for exactly the same time every day. It warned her that she had half an hour. Half an hour to get perfect. Half an hour to breathe.

The routine began. No dust on the furniture; no lint on the carpet; no water spots on the sinks or fixtures; curtains and shades all pulled to exactly the same level and angle; no fingerprints on the door knobs; magazines stacked neatly with all their edges matched; chairs pushed up to the table, all exactly the same distance apart from the table and from each other; vase centered on the lace doily.

She repeated the routine daily, the last minute checklist, to make certain that everything would be just so when he came home. She tried hard to keep from letting any imperfections creep in. Water spots. Yesterday it had been water spots. She wiped at them extra hard today. Even so, she knew that he'd find something. Somehow, he always did. She tried so hard to please him. She did everything she could think of, she tried to be good, but always there was this feeling of hopelessness and fear. He'd find something. He'd find *something* and then she'd be in trouble.

She was nervous as she walked to the window, biting her fingernails, and looked down at the park across the street. Such a nice place, all green and pretty. She watched the children playing—so happy and carefree. She looked at all the young mothers; watching their children at play, not at home fixing dinner; not making sure everything in their homes and in their own appearances was perfect; not afraid. She felt herself getting angry, so she watched the children instead.

The pain was bad today. It was worse than usual. She wished that today would be different. It was her birthday and she had been praying really hard that it would be a good day. She had even dreamed about it last night. She wasn't hoping for gifts. She just wished that he would be nice today, the way he could be sometimes. She wished he'd take her out for pizza, or a movie, or maybe have a party for her. She knew he'd never have a party, though. If he did, he would have to let people into the apartment, and he *never* let people into the apartment. She wasn't allowed to have friends over. She wasn't allowed to have friends at all. Still, she hoped he would be nice. She'd tried extra hard today to make sure the apartment was perfect. Now it was time to make herself perfect.

She went to her room, careful not to cast even a glance at the door across the hall. Everything was in its place, but she smoothed the pink bedspread over the pillow again, just to be sure. She lifted the music box beside her bed and set it in motion. There used to be two of them, Mickey and Minnie. Now she only had Mickey. She had to be very careful not to make him angry so that Mickey didn't get broken too. At the mirror she inspected her reflection. She hated her hair. She wished it were brown again, or red maybe. And she'd really like to cut it into one of the short bouncy styles she looked at in his magazines or like the one worn by the woman in the photograph she'd never met. But he liked it long, and he liked it blonde.

Her dress was fresh, changed just before the alarm went off so it wouldn't be wrinkled when he got there. He wanted her to wear dresses; he wanted her to look like a lady. This one was his favorite. She wanted so badly to please him, especially today, and not just in bed.

Dull blue eyes stared back at her from the mirror. She knew that he loved her. He said so. He told her she was beautiful, he touched her and kissed her. He told her she pleased him too. But all these things were only true in bed. She only wanted his approval and wished he would be pleased with her in other ways as well. She wished he would love her just because she *was*, and because of the things she did for him daily. That was why she tried so hard to make everything perfect. If only she could make everything just right; if only she could make herself *better*—maybe then he would love her. Maybe then he wouldn't hurt her.

She checked her dress collar again to make sure that the purple bruises didn't show. He didn't like it when the bruises showed. She checked the clock and the pain in her gut got worse. It was almost time. "Please," she prayed, "please…"

She hurried back to the window. Right on time—he was pulling in. She had timed it many times and she knew it would take him exactly three and a half minutes to get from the carport to the apartment door. It never changed.

She closed her eyes tightly for just a second, and gripped her hands together.

"Please," she prayed again, "just for today, please."

—⟋⟍—

There's a package under his arm, bright paper and ribbons, and her heart surges with hope. The pain in her stomach eases a bit and then intensifies again as she reminds herself to stay calm.

She meets him at the door. It's expected.

In an instant, the big handsome man at the door sweeps her into his arms, lifting her right up off the floor, finding her mouth with his own, even as he twirls her around, kissing her passionately. Barely able to breathe, she responds, as she knows he wants her to, allowing his tongue to chase hers, eventually capturing and controlling it. It's like a well-rehearsed play and she is his little star. She knows her part. He breaks away, nearly breathless, and holds her tightly against him. She can feel the heat and hardness pressing against her and she knows that her dreams of something different are crumbling away.

"Happy birthday, sweetheart," he whispers.

She feels tears in her eyes and knows that if he sees them he'll be angry, so she presses her face into his neck. It tells him all he wants to know and he leads her to the stairs, throwing the package down—forgotten and unopened.

"Are you having a good birthday, honey?" he asks.

"Yes," she answers, managing to sound sincere, as she knows she must. Just as she knows there will be no pizza—just the sex thing.

"Are you happy, angel?" he asks. "I really want you to be happy."

"Yes," she answers, "I'm happy."

There will be no movie—just this.

As they turn at the landing in the stairway, he sweeps her up once again and kisses her with tenderness as he covers the remaining steps and nudges open the door with his foot. She squeezes her eyes shut, but behind closed lids she still sees the door that she tries so hard not to look at all day long. He lays her on the bed that smells like him and she fights the urge to vomit when she feels the dirty sheets she knows he hasn't washed.

She knows there will be no party—only this. *Always*, only this.

"Today is such a special day," he whispers in the only room in which the shades stay pulled all the way down to the window ledges. "I'm glad you're happy. You should be, you know."

She's grateful for the darkness and for his closed eyes. It makes it all a little bit easier when he touches her at last. It helps to not see so well.

"Such a special day," he breathes. "It's not every day that a girl turns seven."

MY MOTHER'S HOUSE

Broken glass from the twisted metal skeleton of a frame crunched under Bev's feet with her first step into the chaos. "Mother?" she called. "Where are you, Mom?"

"What's wrong, Mom?" Josh asked, coming up the steps behind her, backpack over one shoulder and basketball in hand. "Is Grandma okay?"

She held up a hand for quiet. She listened. "I don't know. Wait here."

"Like hell."

"Watch your mouth!" she snapped.

"Fine then." He set his load upon the porch step. "But I'm coming with you."

Together they stepped over the glass and through the foyer and into the living room where Grandma sat on the coffee table naked, attempting to balance the liberated photograph on her sagging breasts.

"Happy birthday!" she called out joyfully when she saw Bev and Josh in the doorway.

Bev's hand flew to her mouth to hide whatever emotion may happen to be the first to reach the surface: humor, revulsion, pain. It was all there. It was always all there.

"Hey, Gram!" Josh smiled next to Bev. "How they hangin' today?"

"Josh!" Bev snapped, but before her, the subject of her dismay giggled like a schoolgirl and rocked back and forth with the family picture precariously balanced.

"Happyhappyhappyhappyhappyhappyhappyhappyhappy…"

Josh moved around the coffee table to the bedroom door and took the flannel robe off the hook.

"It's a cake!" She grinned up at Josh as he slipped back in to stand beside her.

"Sure is, Gram, but it's only half decorated. Here we go." He said smoothly, slipping the robe around her shoulders and pulling it down. "Now, isn't that better?"

She looked down at the purple and pink plaid and grinned back at him. "It sure is, Walter. You always know just what to do."

Bev watched as Josh took his grandmother's face between his hands and tipped it up to kiss her forehead, both of them smiling—and choked on—something; a laugh, a sob—it could have been either. As always, Josh amazed her, stepping in to do the best thing; the thing her mother needed right at that moment, with ease. She was never that easy with her mother. Josh took the high road, cajoling her out of her bad moods, joining her in her ridiculously good moods, like now, and pretending to be whomever his grandmother believed him to be at the moment, never disagreeing with her. Bev couldn't do it. She missed her mother. It was getting worse. And while Josh distracted what once was her mom; her best friend; she was left to clean up the mess and worry about what to do and how long they could live like this.

Bev looked around the living room. Only the frame in the foyer was broken, but every picture and painting in sight had been taken down. They neatly lined the walls along the baseboards throughout the living and dining rooms and short connecting hallway. Bev stepped to her mother's bedroom door. The same thing here. And the kitchen, the longer hallway, her room, Josh's. She returned to the living room to see Josh tying the belt of the robe around his grandmother's waist. She watched for a moment.

"So, Mom..." she began, "what's up? Cleaning walls today, were you?"

"No. Why would I be cleaning the walls? Maria can do that."

"Maria?" Josh asked with a glance back at Bev. "Who's Maria, Gram?"

"That Spanish girl I hired to clean. Honestly, Walter! You never remember anything. I hired Maria when Sonja got knocked up by that no-good doctor who was married to her sister. For Heaven's sake!"

Josh grinned again. "Oh, *that* Maria. How silly of me."

Bev couldn't help smiling. Her mom couldn't tell her fifteen-year-old grandson from her husband who had been dead for twenty-one years, but she could quote her favorite soap opera verbatim. "So," she asked, "why did Maria take off without finishing the job? Now we'll have to put all these pictures back up ourselves."

"Oh no! No!" She shook her head violently. "You can't put them back up. That's where they hide you know. Behind the pictures."

"Who does?"

"The people."

"What people, Mom?"

"The ones who are trying to rob me. They hide behind the pictures until I turn my back and then they come out and they steal everything that's not nailed down. They steal the food. They take it, they eat it all. There's not a thing to eat, you know. They got it all. Everything except the cake."

"Thank God they didn't get the cake," Josh put in, hugging her again. "Way to go saving the cake, Gram. You're the best."

The mess was cleaned up, pictures stacked in a closet, everyone rooted in for the night. Bev sat alone at the kitchen table with a cold cup of coffee and a stack of papers she'd read a dozen times or more. *Pine Glen Care Center: Haven of the Golden Years.*

In reality, a run down but friendly establishment with no Pines in sight; two person rooms with an awful lot of yelling when she had toured; bland looking food; antiseptic smell; people drooling, pissing, crapping up their bed clothes, and—

Bev lowered her head to her folded arms. How many more times could she clean up her mother's messed bed and nightclothes, let alone her day clothes? Could she go on coming home to even minor disasters, like today's, and then go on with her work, her son, the day-to-day business of living like *normal* ever visited her for more than an hour at a time? Would that vise on her heart tighten every single time her mother didn't recognize her, thought she was someone else, screamed in fright believing that Bev was some marauding stranger who had broken in to harm her?

She pulled the papers closer without lifting her head. She knew them by heart. The pen was in her hand when she heard her mother call and she stopped. What had she said? She lifted her head and listened for the sound to come again.

"Beverly? Beverly?"

She arose slowly and walked in silence to her mother's bedroom door. In the streaks of moonlight shining through the Venetian blinds she could see the reclined silhouette. She waited.

"Beverly, is that you?"

"I'm here, Mom." She waited. "Are you okay? Do you need something?"

A thin hand patted the mattress beside the shadow and Bev stepped to her. She sat gingerly on the side of the bed and picked up the hand.

"I'm sorry I'm such a burden, Beverly." Her voice was quiet; so quiet.

Bev stroked her mother's hand but couldn't summon the words needed to placate.

Feeling her hand squeezed, she looked down into blue eyes, so much like her own; like Josh's. They were clear in the moonlight, the vagueness replaced with pain, understanding, and knowledge. Seeing the mother she had already lost, Bev reached to stroke the hair back from the beloved face before her.

"I love you, Beverly. I don't tell you that often enough, do I?"

"I love you, Mom," Bev's voice could barely work itself out of her throat. "I really do."

The sigh of sleep reached her ears as the hand lost its hold, and Bev pulled the comforter up and smoothed it over the shadow once again. She stayed beside the bed for many minutes, lost in memory. *She's in there... sometimes; she's still in there.*

The time for Pine Glen is coming, she knows. It's coming fast. Bev takes a sip of her coffee, grimaces at the cold bitterness, and pours it down the sink. She eyes the stack of papers with the pen on top and rubs her eyes. She is so damn tired. The papers fold easily as they've been folded so many times. She runs a thumbnail along the crease and puts them back into a kitchen cabinet behind the spices and cornstarch. Pine Glen is coming. But today is not the day.

THE LAST NIGHT

They undressed. Adam tossed his wrinkled jeans and sweatshirt into a corner that was already overflowing with discards as Catherine folded her skirt and silk blouse and carefully hung them over the back of a chair; one of the few places where her clothes might be safe from the dog hair. Above her, a twelve-point buck, a Canadian moose, and a largemouth bass looked down with glassy-eyed stares. A Miller-Lite sign blinked off and on in dubious welcome, hung in between posters of Jim Morrison in a state of semi-dress and an even less dressed adolescent female sprawled across the hood of a silver Corvette. She ought to leave—but…. She had the same disagreement with herself about half-way through his kitchen every time. The Catherine who wanted to stay had the last word. Again. As always, drawn to his clear blue eyes and easy smile with those dimples that she couldn't resist touching, she stayed. Brawny and masculine, not at all her type, he let her.

They lay in his bed, arms and legs entangled; skin damp and clinging; breathing labored; hearts pounding. Adam's hand caressed her long chestnut hair and placed tiny, soft kisses all over her face. She didn't move. She marveled at the way he could do that. He touched her and kissed her in the most loving and passionate ways and then told her again that he could never love her. *It's only sex,* he would say.

For two years, they'd been best friends. They could talk with each other about anything, or at least they used to, until they started sleeping together. Lately, she wished more and more that they'd never crossed that line in their friendship. But both of them had been hurting and lonely. It was only natural. It was strange that they were so close because, really, they had so little in common. She'd often wondered why she was even with him. Maybe because he always listened, even when she was being a bitch, and he could always make her laugh. And then of course there was the sex; the best, most incredible sex.

For a year she'd avoided other men, sure that one day Adam would love her the way that she loved him, but she'd finally come to accept that it wasn't going to happen. He seemed to know all along that she didn't belong in his world any more than he belonged in hers.

"Adam?"

"Hmmm?"

"I met someone."

He stopped kissing her; his hand paused on the back of her hair for the length of a heartbeat then continued its stroking.

"Who is he? Anyone I know?"

"No. I met him at work. He's nice—I think." She didn't know if she should keep talking or wait for him to say something.

"Did he ask you out?"

"Not yet. But he's going to, I can tell."

"And what will you say when he does?"

They'd had this conversation before, but before it had been hypothetical. He kept telling her that she had to keep an open mind in case she met someone. He kept telling her not to love him, too. But she couldn't help that.

He ran his fingers up and down her bare arm and she felt the tingling sensations begin again that he generated in her body with even the most innocent touch. Every hair on her arm prickled in anticipation. God, this was so difficult. She put both arms around him and held him tightly, burying her face against the firm, comfortable warmth of his chest, feeling as if this was where she belonged—yet knowing that it wasn't.

"I don't know," she finally answered him, her voice barely above a whisper. "I'm scared."

"What are you scared of?"

"Everything! Him. You. Me. I don't want to go through this again."

"Go for it. What have you got to lose?"

She laughed, but the sound was without mirth. "What have I got to lose? Oh, that's a good one coming from you."

"Come on, Cath," he said, pulling her up with him until their backs were leaning against the cold plaster of the wall and his warm arm was draped over her shoulders. "Listen, I know what we have isn't enough for you. It isn't enough for me either, but it's all I can handle right now. We've both known for a long time that eventually one of us would meet someone else and we'd have to have the talk we're having tonight."

She tried to turn her head away from him but he pulled her closer. The light filtering in from the street lamps cut horizontal shadows across their faces.

"Shh," he whispered, kissing her softly. "Don't cry, Cath, please? I can't stand to see you cry."

"I love you."

"I know."

It never changed. She'd only said it a few times, but whenever she did, his reply was the same: *I love you.* "I know."

He held her, absorbing the shudders of her body with his own, until there was nothing left, until she just rested quietly in his arms.

"So. Are you ready to stop that blubbering and tell me about this guy, or what?" He poked at her, using the teasing tone that he turned on whenever things got too serious between them.

She couldn't help smiling, and when he poked her again, knowing all too well where her ticklish spots were, she laughed and slid out of his arms back down, under the covers. He followed her, capturing both her hands and pulling them up to his face. He kissed them each once and looked at her with his eyes sparkling. God, he loved to give her a hard time.

"Come on," he prodded, "tell me all about him."

"Okay." She couldn't look at him, so she focused on her hands, still locked in his. "His name is Marc, and he's as different from you as any two people could possibly be."

"How's that?"

"Well, he's smart for one thing, *he* likes me."

The pillow hit her on the side of the head before she even saw it coming, then he caught her by both arms and pinned her to the mattress. They were both laughing and breathless for a moment. Their laughter subsided and they looked into each other's eyes. His caught the outside light, which failed to give them the sparkle she'd come to expect; hers were shrouded in shadow that hid the sorrow she suddenly felt. For moments there was no sound in the room except that of their quick breaths returning to normal.

"You're jealous."

"I wish I were. But I'm not."

"Then what is it?"

"Am I going to lose you?" His eyes looked gray in the muted light. "I don't know what I'd do without you in my life at all."

She touched his face. They looked at each other. She didn't know who else she could ever talk to like this. She feared she'd never know another man she could trust in the way that she trusted Adam.

He wondered who would be there for him if she left, and was afraid for the first time in his life of being alone.

But when she looked at the clutter around her and compared it to her own ordered life, she knew she had to go…and when he inhaled her expensive perfume that he couldn't even afford, he knew he had to let her. He'd never learn to love the theatre and she'd never learn to bait a hook. She'd go on reading poetry and he'd keep playing pool at Hard Times on Friday nights. It wasn't anyone's fault…it's just the way things were.

—⚉—

Much later, they stood beneath the light on the sagging porch littered with softball equipment. The house could use a coat of paint and the cluttered yard should have been mowed one more time before the leaves had fallen. Catherine smiled at the mess and rested the top of her head on Adam's chest, looking down at his bare feet. He ran his fingers through her hair. They couldn't seem to stop touching each other, and they both knew why.

"Well, I guess it's time—I really should go."

"Yeah, I guess you should."

Adam tilted her face and brushed back the hair from it, taking in the heavy, dark beauty of her and the deep mahogany of her sad eyes. He kissed her forehead, his hands cradling her cheeks.

"Go for it Cath. Give the guy a break. He can't be as big an asshole as I am."

"That's true."

They smiled and held each other for a moment until he pulled away to look at her and saw the determination in her face—he knew the time had come to let her go.

"Just do it."

"I will." She hesitated on the words she had to say. "But Adam?"

"Yeah?"

"If I do, and it works out—I won't be back."

He managed a smile and touched her face gently. "I know."

They kissed, then smiled at each other, and she turned and walked down the steps toward her clean, sensible Buick, parked next to his rusty old pickup with the duck boat already anchored to the roof. He'd be hunting in the morning while she was having her first cup of coffee in front of her computer.

—⚏—

"Cath," his voice stopped her. She turned and looked back at him, across the leaf-strewn yard, with their breaths hanging between them on the cold, autumn air, and she waited. "I really do love you."

She answered him in the only way she could, "I know."

KISS

Her head was pressed against the wall, her face upraised, her left arm twined around his waist and her hand gripping the fabric of his jacket in a tightly balled fist. In her right hand she clutched a single red rose against her hip.

He leaned into her; a bag slung over one shoulder, freeing both arms for the business at hand. And the kiss went on.

I watched from a reasonably comfortable seat at gate 23 while I was waiting for my flight to be announced. It was mesmerizing, that kiss. A guilty twinge told me that it was unfair to stare at them, yet I couldn't tear my gaze away.

She was tall and slim, nearly as tall as he. Some precocious static on the textured wall held her blonde hair and fanned it out and around the crown of her head like a nimbus, until he spread his fingers through it, spoiling the lovely effect.

He wasn't young. Older than I, probably, with brown hair markedly thinner than his rangy build. There was, however, a passion about him that caught and held my attention.

Yes, of course they were older; middle aged by most standards; old enough to know how to kiss properly anyway. Young people don't know how to kiss. Not really. Oh the mechanics are all the same, I suppose, but the *style*—ah, therein lies the difference. I teach high school, so I know. Watching teenagers kiss is akin to watching monster mud trucks or all-star wrestling. The adrenaline rush is undoubtedly there, but it's just not a pretty sight.

Sitting at gate 23, I looked around me. People were engrossed in conversations and in magazines as others rushed on by—hurrying to their destinations, as if the earth weren't moving just ten feet away.

They broke apart and looked deeply at each other for a moment and, for the first time, I could see her clearly. She was lovely, but her face was streaked with tears.

Who are they? I wondered. *What's their story?* Everyone has a story, and some just cry out to be told. Since I couldn't very well walk up to two strangers, tap them on their shoulders, and *ask* them—I began to concoct my own.

He's just returned from the Mayo Clinic where he has been diagnosed with a brain tumor and will die in six months.

They've just endured a trial separation and have now, only this moment, realized that they're each no good without the other.

There's been a death—someone close—they're mourning together. Yes. That's it. There's something decidedly comforting in that embrace.

Maybe he's just proposed. No. Her expression is too sad for that.

He's a soldier off to war, a salesman to sell, a musician to perform, a doctor, a lawyer, a foreign diplomat who wears jeans and a leather jacket to downplay his importance.

For some reason, none of my scenarios felt right.

Her face was pressed deeply into his neck and she held him now with both arms, just as he held her—the rose's petals against her nose. They kissed again, angling their bodies and lips together for a tighter, more satisfying fit. Still, no one else seemed to notice because their quiet passion was so unobtrusive; it's balletic intimacy catching only my attention.

My curiosity grew as the kiss lengthened. Neither of them was in a hurry to get anywhere and so they were loathe to part. Parting seemed to be the catalyst for the tears and sorrow. He had to be leaving, for if he were arriving, wouldn't they be happy? Wouldn't they be rushing off to a private place to share this moment?

They parted once more, and though I had yet to look upon his face, hers spoke volumes. Whatever was wrong, it was no small thing. Her tears flowed freely as she lifted both of his hands to her face and kissed them, first one then the other, lingeringly, with her eyes closed. She pressed her cheek once more to his and turned her face into his hair— breathing as if to inhale his very being into the tapestry of her own soul.

He tried to kiss her again, but she held him at arm's length. She attempted to smile, failed miserably, then walked away backward, leaving—to my surprise—the red rose, tucked tightly under the lapel of his leather jacket.

She disappeared into the crowd and he turned, placing both palms flat on the wall where she had stood. Minutes passed, and still he stood.

What love! I thought. *Where does it come from? What power it has to move people this way—even I—a lonely observer.*

Finally, he turns, a plain man; an ordinary face, but kind—I am certain. A man—I am sure—with as much compassion as passion. He understands her pain, and maybe even *mine* in a strange sort of way, because he is obviously harboring so much of his own.

He looks toward me, but not *at* me. He takes the rose from his lapel and looks at it as if it were a living, breathing thing, instead of a dead stem, plucked from a growing bush. He lowers his head with his eyes closed and leans back against the wall.

At the gate next to mine a flight has arrived and people crowd forward to claim their loved ones. He slowly moves away from the wall. I watch.

Suddenly a little girl, about five or so, breaks from the crowd and races toward him. "Daddy!" she shouts.

I'm surprised to see him drop to his knees as the tiny body propels itself into his arms. He smiles and kisses her hair. His lips are moving although I can't hear the words.

He stands with her arms and legs wrapped so tightly around his body that he need not even hold her—yet he does. He breathes in the scent of this child with a desperate, pained expression—much as the woman had breathed in his. His eyes are closed against the noise and color surrounding them.

The child squeals and reaches toward a pretty, auburn haired woman whose smile is radiant as she approaches the pair. With one hand on the child's back and the other on the man's neck, she kisses his lips. It is a kiss of *hello, I love you, I've missed you, I trust you*—not passion filled, but poignant—and it too moves me.

They turn to go and I find my heart both empty and full, understanding and confused. What agonies we subject ourselves to—we human animals—what liberties we take with each other's hearts!

As they pass, never breaking their three-way embrace, our eyes meet, his and mine. It is like looking into a trick mirror where I see both what I am and what I could never be at the same time. I see myself clearly in my solitude and, for the first time, I am grateful for it. No one cries for me tonight, nor I for them. But somewhere in this dreary city a woman cries—the tapestry of her soul undone—and another woman smiles and hurries toward home with a man who hands to her a single red rose.

A BROWN LEATHER JACKET WITH A DISTINCTIVE SMELL

He only had three moods: uncommunicative, amorous, and pissed off. None of them were pleasant, but there are degrees, you know? Pissed off is what finally drove me away—because pissed off meant pissed on and was only one step removed from homicidal. Not a *large* step, you understand. Of course, amorous wasn't much better. Amorous was actually pissed off under a veneer of intense desire that could never be satiated, whereby it evolved into pissed off. Are you following me? Now, uncommunicative I could live with—provided I was willing to live tippy-toeing on eggshells, because uncommunicative was really just pissed off in the larva stage. Hmmm. I guess he really didn't have *three* moods after all.

He did have another face though. His fake face. The one he wore on special occasions—like when he wanted something and needed my undivided attention, which, of course, I would give—kind of like the way flies give their undivided attention to dead, rotting flesh when it lies on the roadside under the hot summer sun. Ah yes. He could be quite charming. At least *he* thought so. I don't think he realized that I saw through him when he was being "sweet." I think he thought I bought his act. I'm *sure* he thought I bought it. He thought I was incredibly stupid—and for a while, he was right.

Actually, my worst memories are attached to his sweet side, because everything else was pretty predictable, like the hipbone connected to the thighbone, there was a certain symmetry to his madness. "Sweet" was scarier really, because the hipbone *might* be connected to the thighbone, but on the other hand, the hipbone might be connected to the shoulder bone, and then all bets are off. Are you still with me?

Now, I guess you're asking yourself, "What the hell does all this have to do with the brown leather jacket with a distinctive smell?" Right? Well, I'm getting to it. Don't rush me.

Anyway, there was always that last moment, right before he came through the door each evening—that moment charged with dread, hope, and prayer. But for what? When you know that a man has no good side—only variations of his *bad* side—just what is it you dread, and hope, and pray for? It's a horrible, empty feeling to pray when you don't know exactly what it is you're praying for—except for the one deep desire you're afraid to voice—that he doesn't come home at all. That he falls madly in love with Ilsa, the buxom, blonde barmaid at the *Gute Nacht Pub,* and they run away together. Or better yet, that he's been in a terrible accident and his broken body is lying on Autobahn Five between Hanau and Neuenhasslau—dead. Only he didn't just die. No. He suffered in mindless, screaming agony for an eternity of seconds before finally succumbing to the Grim Reaper who had surely carted him off to hell by now...but wait, I digress. Forgive me. I shouldn't let the daily fantasies I entertain interfere with the point at hand: that *particular* evening, and the brown leather jacket with the distinctive smell.

I was standing at the kitchen sink, a potato in one hand and a peeler in the other. I used to love the smell of fresh raw potatoes as I peeled them. *Now* I don't notice if they even *have* a smell. They don't make potatoes like they used to. There was a beef roast in the oven at 375-degrees. *It* smelled pretty good. Onions and bay leaves help, you know? I'd peeled four carrots and three potatoes. Three and a half, technically, when I heard his key in the door.

"Hi honey, it's me," he yelled. *Like, who the hell else would it be?*

"I'm in the kitchen," I yelled back. *Shit, he wasn't lying dead on the Autobahn.*

I heard a thunk as his briefcase hit the coffee table in the living room and a softer thump of something else that didn't quite register at the time. I started on a fourth potato.

He came through the kitchen door and I gave him my practiced Donna Reed smile that said, "I'm so glad you're home." *You fucking son of a bitch.* His arms came around me from behind and his chin rested heavily on my shoulder as his paws settled on my breasts.

Amorous, I thought. *Shit.* I tried to remember the last time he'd touched my face, hand, shoulders, arms, or neck. This isn't your romantic kind of guy who offers sweet touches, kind words, or tokens of esteem. Nor is he your settled, boring husband who needs encouragement—you now—a little jump-start now and then? No. This is a move in for the kill kind of guy; a guy whose idea of foreplay is, "Wake up, bitch," at three a.m. So, his hands on my tits in point zero three seconds was really no surprise.

"What's for dinner?" he whispered in what I figured was supposed to be a sexy voice.

"Roast," I answered, in what I hoped *wasn't.*

"Mmmm…" he murmured, as his hands slid down the front of my blouse and over the zipper on my jeans. One hand slipped between my legs and his fingers pressed up against my crotch. He probably thought he was turning me on, but the word *finesse* was not in his vocabulary. Actually, he was hurting me. He pressed too hard for too long and the denim seam cut into me—but I didn't react. It was one thing I'd learned early. Don't react. If I faked pleasure, he'd press harder. If I showed pain, he'd press harder. If I expressed any displeasure, he'd press harder *and* I'd be forcing the evolution of amorous to pissed off.

He bit my neck. It hurt. I didn't react.

"Well hurry up, woman," he said. "I'm starving." He backed away from me, taking his offensive paws with him. I held my breath, expecting it. He didn't disappoint me. The slap across my backside stung with intense reverberations that spread clear up to my ears. My stomach and one hip bumped hard against the edge of the sink, but otherwise I didn't move, didn't flinch. You'd think it would have been toughened up by then. The slap was so predictable. It was part of the pattern, you see. The hipbone connected to the thighbone. He walked out. I sighed. Patterns.

The television clicked on, too loud, as usual. I gauged the evolutionary time frame: the usual pattern, add four, carry the two, consider all variables, subtract one, oil the joints, and assume the thighbone is still connected to the knee bone, add one dinner, subtract four—or maybe five—Bacardis, and what have you got? Who the hell knows?

"Jenny!" he screamed at me from the living room. "Get your ass in here."

I jumped. It appeared that man was about to become ape slightly ahead of schedule.

I dropped the potato and the peeler and ran to the living room. He was mad. So what? He was always mad. But something was different—something in his eyes, his stance—I was so used to him that I didn't really get *scared* anymore, but at that moment, I did. Of course, I didn't show it.

"What's wrong?"

"What's wrong? What's *wrong?!*" He laughed. "*This* is what's wrong, you fucking slut!" He raised his hand, and I saw it for the first time, clutched in his talons: a brown leather jacket.

I felt a brief moment of relief. After all, what was so terrible about a jacket?

"What the fuck is this?" A purple vein was pulsating in his forehead.

"A jacket?" I guessed.

"You smartass little bitch!" he shouted. "*A jacket?*" He mimicked my innocent question. "Yes, it's a jacket! It's a Goddamn jacket, you slut!" He moved toward me menacingly and raised the jacket above his head.

The first blow fell on the top of my head with one well-worn sleeve hitting my shoulder. It didn't hurt me at all, and for some reason—I really don't know why—that made me smile. His rage was instantaneous, and I did something unthinkable: I *laughed.*

He made a sound like a wounded animal, pulled the jacket back and swung it again, this time—across my face. I stopped laughing.

He reared back and swung again, landing blow after blow across my face with the jacket, each one stinging more than the last as the leather slapped against skin that was progressively rawer and more tender. I held my arms up in a futile effort to shield my face.

"Whose is it, slut?" He didn't wait for a reply—or want one. "Who the hell's been here while I'm out working, huh? Who the hell did you fuck in my bed, whore?"

The jacket's zipper bit into my cheek and a metal stud hit my closed eyelid. A searing pain shot from my eye to the back of my head and I dropped to my knees. I felt blood on my face and could only see red through my left eye.

"I don't know, I don't know," I kept repeating. "I swear to God, I don't know. No one was here—please believe me. I swear to God, I've never seen that jacket before. I swear I don't know, I don't know."

He didn't listen. He didn't hear. He didn't know that I tippy-toed on eggshells to avoid confrontations. He didn't know that I was telling the truth. That I'd never seen that jacket before. That no one had been there—that day or any day. He didn't know that not only would I never cheat on him—but that his brand of *love* had cured me of ever wanting a man in my life or in my bed again—*ever!* He didn't know. He didn't hear. And he didn't listen.

Everything was gray and red and it didn't hurt anymore. His voice sounded distant and tinny—like he was shouting into a rain barrel with the same old refrain: "Bitch...who is he? Slut...do you think I'm stupid? Whore...you lousy, cheating whore!" He was still swinging, but for some reason, it just didn't hurt anymore.

I must not have turned the water tap tight enough, I thought, for I could hear a steady dripping sound. Then someone down the block started a lawn mower and I couldn't hear it anymore. The grayness became darker and my face was so wet. *Am I crying?* I wondered. *I never cry... I would never give him that satisfaction again.* I forced my right eye open. It was against the carpet, and my eyelash brushed against the rough fibers. His left foot was by my face. He'd taken off his shoes and I noticed how small that foot was. I remember thinking that for a tough guy, he sure had wimpy feet. And it smelled—a smelly foot smell—and as I took breaths between blows I kept getting a nose full of his disgusting foot smell. But then I got smart. I started *exhaling* between blows.

The jacket came down on my head, and as a sleeve fell across my face, I inhaled deeply, causing the leather to cling for a second to my nose and open mouth. I did it again and again. It was old leather. It had a rugged smell—not the stifling smell of wools or tweeds. I smelled different cologne, one I'd never smelled before. It was a piney odor that for a brief moment, made me think that I was outside, lying on the grass under the pines in my parents' backyard. It was comforting and exciting—not cloying, like the accustomed musk-scent.

I breathed and breathed, wanting to suck that jacket into my lungs—to absorb the leather into the fabric of my own being. I wanted that smell, that wonderful distinctive smell, to stay with me forever.

Suddenly I remembered the sound I'd heard when he first came home—the sound of him putting something down in the living room—and I knew. *He brought it here, the sick bastard!* He was beating me as a part of some sick game that only he knew the rules to. I never found out whom that jacket belonged to, and I don't suppose I ever will, but as I huddled there, I knew something more important—that he had brought it into our *home* to punish me for a crime that had only happened in his sick mind.

I don't know if he kept hitting me after I passed out or if he'd finally had enough of the game by that time, but it really doesn't matter…because as the gray became black, I had only one thought. It wasn't dread, or hope, or a prayer. I didn't wish for him to run away with Ilsa the

barmaid, or to die on the Autobahn. No. My only thought was *freedom...*
emancipation... and a brown leather jacket with a distinctive smell—one
that I hadn't known in a long, long time. The distinctive smell was my
life... and I took that jacket with me when I left.

BLOOD SISTERS

He came awake slowly, luxuriating in those mindless moments between sleep and wakefulness, vaguely aware of a warm wetness tracing a river up his spine. Ah, Melody. He slipped into consciousness as remembrance dawned and he smiled. What a woman! Horny as hell already and the sun was barely up.

Her tongue had worked its magical way up to his neck where it flicked playfully at the underside of his hair. If only Amanda had a fraction of Melody's finesse. But his sexy secretary knew tricks that his innocent little wife just didn't have a clue about.

Every now and then Michael felt a slight twinge of guilt, like now for instance, but he squelched it. If Amanda could keep him satisfied in bed—and type—he wouldn't need Mel. And if Mel had Amanda's money, he'd get a lawyer tomorrow. Anyway, since they were both too fucking stupid to figure out about each other, he figured they were just getting what they deserved.

"Turn over, darling," she whispered, her tongue flicking in and out of his ear, and her hand sliding forward across his hip to give him incentive that he didn't really need at this point.

My God, but she was good at this. He rolled to his back, eyes still closed in anticipation of her expert love. Any second now he would feel her long blonde hair sweep across his chest and he would reach up and run his fingers through it.

He stretched his hands upward and opened his grainy eyes, trying to focus on the woman straddling his hips, but her hair didn't reach his chest, and it sure as hell wasn't blonde.

"Amanda," he croaked, "wha…how…?"

"Shh, darling." A scarlet tipped finger pressed against his lips. "You had a rough night, Michael. You probably don't even remember, but it's a shame when you spend five hundred bucks on a hotel suite and then get too drunk to even enjoy it."

"But...what did...how do...?" He was losing his mind. Melody. He'd come here with Melody. Dear God, he was losing his mind.

"You fell asleep on me last night, but don't think you're going to get off so easy this morning." She smiled at him, the suggestion clear in her eyes and her words. "Well, let me rephrase that. You'll definitely get off...just not so easy."

Then she went to work on him like she'd never done before. Now he was certain he was losing his mind. She had him clutching the pillow and crying out in ecstasy before he could even make himself believe that it was real.

"What's gotten into you, babe?" His breathing was ragged as he dragged himself to the side of the bed, his limbs shaking. "Where the hell did you learn all that stuff?"

"Oh. I bought a book."

"A book?" He laughed. "Must be some fucking book."

"Oh it is, darling. It definitely is."

Her words were lost on him as he staggered into the bathroom and turned on the shower full blast and as hot as he could stand. Standing beneath the spray of water with shampoo in his hair and running in rivulets down his face, he contemplated the weirdness of the situation. He didn't know how he'd gone to bed with Mel and woke up with Amanda, but he really didn't give a shit. If she could learn all that from a book he'd buy her a fucking library.

He felt the curtain move beside him as she stepped into the shower, pressing her lithe body against his naked back, her hands making circular motions through the soap on his chest, flicking her fingernails at his nipples, then scratching red tracks down his abdomen, lower, and lower.

He held his face to the pounding shower stream and swiped at his eyes with the backs of his hands, but she swung him around to face her before he could clear his vision.

She grabbed his face and kissed him long and hard, sweeping the interior of his mouth with her tongue as if she were seeking his tonsils. While he was still standing with one hand on the wet, tiled wall for balance and wiping frantically at his eyes with the other hand, she tore herself away from his mouth, and hers began its downward journey.

She knelt before him, her tongue stroking, teasing of better things to come, as he finally cleared his eyes enough to open them and peer down through the water and steam.

"Hello, darling."

Oh my God, oh my God, oh my God! Now there could be no doubt he was losing his mind. There was no mistaking that long, silky hair, even hanging in darker, wet tangles around his knees. It was Melody, and she was smiling up at him.

"Remember when you said that I could suck an orange through a garden hose, darling?"

He clutched the wall and the curtain for support and squeezed his eyes shut. What was happening to his mind? And how the hell could he figure it out when she was wreaking such havoc with his body? He should make her stop, but even in his present condition, he wasn't that crazy.

That was it! He wasn't crazy at all. He was just dreaming. Of course. Amanda must have been a dream. That had to be it. It had been Mel all along and his hangover had impaired his comprehension somehow. It all made perfect sense. Melody was here with him like she was supposed to be and Amanda was at home preparing him the usual Sunday feast that he enjoyed so much after his Saturday nights with Mel. It was fucking exhausting.

Melody began working her way back up his body, not missing a single inch of his slippery skin with her soft lips.

"Hurry back, darling. I'll be waiting to finish." She ran her tongue across her lips seductively and whispered, "I can't wait. Don't be too long." Then she gave him that sexy little smirk that never failed to get him revved.

Michael finished scrubbing his body in anxious anticipation. Damn—she was even hornier than usual. He loved it. Nothing could have been further from his mind than the silly dream he'd had about Amanda.

—m—

"Amanda!"

"Michael."

"But…but…"

"Hello Michael."

"Melody!"

He stood dripping, head pounding, ears ringing. Both of them. Both of them? Dear God, both of them!

"Amanda…Mel…I can…I thought…"

"You can *what* Michael? Explain?"

"And you thought *what* Michael? That we'd understand?"

He was floundering. He felt dizzy. There was a film of sweat on his forehead and another forming on his back. They were smiling at each other. Sweet Jesus, they were smiling!

"Oh, by the way, Michael, I didn't buy a book. Mel filled me in on your—shall we say—*preferences*? Did it ever occur to you to just tell me what you'd like? Well? Did it?"

All he could do was stare as they both moved toward him slowly.

"And did it ever occur to you to mention to me that you had a wife, Michael? A very lovely wife?"

"Why, thank you, Mel."

"Don't mention it, Amanda."

They moved in further, still smiling, a hypnotic gleam in their eyes. A flash of light caught Michael's attention and his eyes shot downward. Cleavers! Holy Christ Almighty! They both had cleavers!

Mesmerized by the sight and paralyzed by fear, he could only stare as a low moan of terror began in his throat and the loosely wrapped towel collapsed in a puddle around his feet.

They glanced at the towel, then at each other, smiling.

"Thank you, Michael."

"Yes. That makes it so much easier, doesn't it?"

"Oh it does. It definitely does."

Melody held her cleaver up to the light as Amanda wiped hers gently across her terrycloth encased thigh.

The moan escalated and his eyes rolled back in his skull.

"Would you like to go first?"

"Oh no. You go ahead."

"Are you sure?"

"I insist."

"No. Let's do it together."

"Oh yes, let's! It's fitting."

"It's the way it should be, I think. Don't you?"

"I couldn't agree with you more."

"On three?"

"On three."

They smiled at each other again, as the man before them gazed sightlessly, senselessly at some point beyond their sphere of reality, his mouth hanging slack, and a trickle of spittle dribbling down his chin.

"One...two..."

"You know, I'm really kind of glad this happened."

"Me too. You're like the sister I've never had."

"We're all sisters in the blood, honey."

"Amen."

"Three?"

"Three."

CATCH ME IF YOU CAN

Ingredients:
1 Car
1 Police Officer, more if necessary
1 Cell Phone
A variety of snacks, drinks, etc.
A Book

I drive, as always, too fast: My excuse? Too many miles on the Autobahn...I mean, seriously, America, who needs speed limits? There is a bag of powdered sugar donuts on my lap, Chex Mix on the seat next to me, one Diet Pepsi in my right hand and another in the holder at my right elbow, while I read a novel with a scantily clad couple on the front cover, using my left hand to both hold the book and manage the steering wheel. My cell phone is balanced on my left shoulder as I hold an animated conversation with my sister. Suddenly the cruiser approaching me flips a U-turn as the red and blue lights begin to flash, and with a sigh, I turn the page and continue reading as I screech to a halt on the shoulder, spitting up gravel that pings off the grill of the approaching blue and white.

I roll down the window when the officer taps, telling my sister to hold on a sec, as I look askance at the rather handsome uniformed man above me and offer him a donut. He takes it and asks me if I know why he stopped me—which, of course, I don't!

Ten seconds later, I drive away with a wave, promising to get that taillight fixed right away as I open the second Diet Pepsi—wake up wondering, why can't all traffic stops go this smoothly?!

Monologues

Intended for stage and/or competition

AN AMERICAN NIGHTMARE

A Dramatic Reading

1 Female - Natasha

NATASHA: To have it all...plenty of money, a beautiful house in the suburbs, cars, vacations, a handsome, loving husband with success in his back pocket, polite, intelligent children...***to have it all***....is—The American Dream. And that dream is what brought me to Michael, across oceans and mountains as a new bride, and new American, just a few years ago. I did have it all. Michael had just started a new job, which meant permanent financial security, we'd moved into our perfect home, put Alison into a top-notch kindergarten, and I'd quit my job to stay home with our newborn, Scotty. Life was just about perfect. Then, one day, tragedy struck, and started a chain reaction of events that turned our lives into something very different: not a dream—but an American nightmare.

It was April; we were having an early spring. I opened the door to golden sun, dewy green grass, and the heady scent of lilacs in the air all around me. The fine purple flowers joined with the pale pink hydrangeas and the blue of the delphiniums...turning my front garden into an explosion of color and life.

Speaking of an explosion of color and life...Alison bounded onto the porch beside me, then raced down the walkway. I had dressed her, after breakfast, in an adorable dress of yellow and pink flowers on pale blue cotton. She wore pink ankle socks and little black shoes, with her long blonde hair clipped back with a pink barrette.

I always waited on the porch, since the bus came around the corner from the right and parked across from our house – the red STOP arm promising safety—still...a mother watches. The bus came around the corner and Alison stepped off the curb, turning to wave at me, and then...

71

It happened so fast! I keep going over and over it in my head... replaying it...believing, or trying to, that if I think it often enough and hard enough that I can reach her in time...I can stop that beat up old car from careening around the school bus...I can stop it from hitting my little girl...I can stop that scream...that horrible, heart-wrenching scream that will haunt me all my days. If I could think it often enough and hard enough, I could stop the blood from staining her pink socks and flowered dress, from matting her pretty blonde hair...I could hold my baby one more time.

I did. Hold her, that is. Sitting on the street, sobbing, cradling her broken little body, willing her to keep breathing, to fight, and screaming for help—even after help had arrived. The ambulance wailed, Scotty screamed, I sobbed, and Alison breathed...just barely.

The hours were interminable. Waiting...waiting...I was so cold.

Michael finally came...who had called him? He said I did... I don't remember. We waited together. We cried. We prayed. We took turns holding Scotty.

One surgery...two...Alison hung on. A third surgery and seven pints of blood. She made it through the night, comatose. For three days and three nights we kept our vigil, Michael and I. Through four surgeries, two transfusions, forty-two signatures, breathing tubes, feeding tubes, oxygen, straps across her tiny body on the sterile white bed, seventy-three cards, eighteen floral arrangements, six teddy bears, and a balloon.

On the fourth morning, Alison left us. Just slipped away...out of her pain, while ours was just beginning.

I supplied Carson's Funeral Home with Alison's favorite dress, all the colors of the rainbow; *dear God...can this be real?* new white tights and shoes.

Carson's Funeral Home supplied us with the most ridiculously tiny coffin I had ever seen... *Sleep, my darling...sleep...*powder blue, with brass handles and white satin lining.

Helen Johansen sang *Child of....oh God, don't take her, please.*

Reverend Denton said to cherish fond memories... but all I feel is pain.

Ashes to ashes, dust to dust...my baby girl to the cold, cold ground. *Why? Oh God, why?*

Days blurred together into nothingness. Despair descended to replace the numbness in our lives. The bills from Alison's last days started pouring in, and despondently, we filed insurance claims daily.

"Dear Mr. Anderson," the letter began, "We regret to inform you that the claim you have submitted is invalid for coverage. If you would refer to your policy, paragraph 6, sub paragraph d, you will see that your coverage begins 180 days after your first day of employment. Regretfully, the incident in question and subsequent medical bills, occurred beginning on the 166th day of your employment, and therefore are not covered by your present policy. It is, however, in effect now, which, I'm sure will be of some consolation to you. At this time, you are responsible for the entire billed amount of 326-thousand 6-hundred 44-dollars and 78-cents."

The rest of the letter swam before my eyes. No insurance? How could it be?

Michael phoned the insurance company—went to the insurance company—was thrown out of the insurance company for overturning the manager's desk. He went to his own employers for help. For weeks he tried. We met with much sympathy but no help and no satisfaction.

We put our house on the market and I began looking for a job. I started working nights as a cashier at a grocery store. Michael spent nights with Scotty and I spent days—while neither of us slept. We applied for a loan. We were turned down.

I returned to our house at midnight one night to find police cars and an ambulance parked in our driveway—lights flashing. Neighbors in bathrobes were peering at me—at the house—Oh God! What now? Don't you know that I can't take anymore?

A large police officer stopped me when I tried to enter the house, and Sandy—my next-door neighbor—came toward me carrying

Scotty in her arms and pain on her face. A covered stretcher coming out the front door onto the porch—NO!! NO!! This can't be happening!!! MICHAEL!!!! It was as if I were mired in mud to my hips. I tried to move…to speak…but I couldn't. Joe, Sandy's husband, had heard the shot and come over…had found Michael. He had called the police and the ambulance.

(Changing voice and demeanor briefly)

Don't go in there. You shouldn't see it. Do you have someplace you and Scotty can go tonight? Excuse me, ma'am…was your husband depressed?

(Returns to self)

SHUT UP!! SHUT UP!!! *(She breaks down)* Damn you, Michael! Who the hell do you think you are, leaving me to face this all alone? We'd have worked it all out eventually. We'd have survived. We had Scotty. We had each other. You selfish son of a bitch! Oh Michael. Ali. Michael.

(She pauses and regains some control)

"Dear Mrs. Anderson. We regret to inform you that death by suicide voids the life insurance policy of your husband of which you are the beneficiary. If you would refer to page 4, paragraph 2….."

TRAINING

A Dramatic Reading

1 Female - Jen

JEN: "One, two, three"—and we jumped. Adrenaline pumped, pulses raced, we hit the metal rungs simultaneously and the rumble of the train shimmied up from my feet to the hair on my head.

We couldn't hear each other over the roar of the great iron wheels rumbling down the track and the occasional piercing cry of the whistle, so we'd long since given up trying, but Liz gave me a grinning thumbs up. I hung back from the racing boxcar as far as my curled fingers and toes would allow, giving the wind free reign at my hot cheeks. *(Jen pantomimes holding the rungs and leaning back, eyes closed)*

I was thirteen and a half. Liz had just turned. We'd been doing this two or three times a month in good weather since we were eleven. A few other kids had tried it. Luther Watts had made it once but he fell backwards and scared the hell out of everybody. So then

Liz and I continued to do it alone.

Liz moved to Checawe when we were in second grade. She lived on the wrong side of the tracks. That's what my mom said. I never really understood what made one side right and one side wrong, but it was true that she lived on the *other* side from me, and once we got past that first winter when she tried to steal my ice skates by writing her name over mine in permanent marker, we were friends. Sort of. I didn't know why my mom didn't like her, and the wind blew just as coldly on me at her house.

(Jen begins to move, wanting to share her story fully with the entire audience, and wanting the audience to understand and be part of her excitement)

I was fascinated by trains; always had been. When I was six, my sister, Margaret, and her friend Julie let me walk with them across the trestle when there was only a single track and the thrill of the risk enticed me even then. Later, I would sit alone on the bank at the edge of town where the north and southbound tracks met and just watch. The conductor would blow the whistle and wave whenever he saw me. The rumble warmed my body and the whistle always sounded lonely and beckoning, like I belonged somewhere else and didn't know why.

Liz felt it too. Or she *said* she did. I loved the trains. I think that she just liked taking risks. The first time I did it, she dared me to jump as the boxcars passed.

"Just jump," she said. "Just jump up and grab the ladder on the side and see how long you can hang on."

When I hesitated, she added, "What's the matter? You chicken?"

One thing I was not, even at eleven, or ever, was a chicken. And I've always been a sucker for a dare. So I took off—barefoot, running alongside the lumbering train, gravel scraping my summer-calloused soles. I could feel the train's rhythm in my heartbeat. I could smell oil and steam and freshly mown grass, and for just a moment I worried that the ladder rungs might be slippery. *(Jen throws out her arms, almost in ecstasy – then goes into a realistic pantomime)* Then I was airborne. My right hand closed over the third rung and I swung myself up, curled the toes of both feet around the lowest rung, and then reached higher with my left. It was just that simple and I was climbing toward the top. I looked back and saw Liz, hands on hips, slack-jawed stupid, standing in my dust—and I shouted for joy. Face to the wind, I stretched back to feel the full extent of the freedom of flying my own boxcar. "See how long you can hang on," she'd said. Are you kidding?! I could hang on forever! But I didn't know where the train was going, so I jumped, making sure to clear the tracks by a good margin and rolled in the dirt. Then I lay flat on my back and stared up at the hazy sun, feeling like I'd just conquered the world.

I heard her feet kicking up the gravel and her lungs working on overtime, but I didn't look back. She called out but I ignored her, closing my eyes and absorbing the vibrations of the fast disappearing train in the muscles of my legs and back.

"Are you okay? Did you fall?" She actually sounded concerned.

I laughed and finally looked at her. "So…you chicken, or what?"

"God! You scared me." She fell prone beside me. "So, how was it? Were you freaked or what?

"It was awesome. It was the coolest thing I ever did in my life." *(Jen laughs and stretches her arms toward the sky)* "I'd have stayed on if I'd known where I could jump and take the southbound back."

"That's easy." Liz said. "You could take this seven miles to the Summit underpass, hang out for about half an hour and take the southbound back. It would be so quick, no one would even miss us."

"Us?"

"Us. Tomorrow. Here. 3:30."

(Jen begins to move again, including everyone in her memoir with a combination of innocence and passion that should be infectious)

That was how it started. The 3:30 northbound, just out of sight of the depot. Seven miles of wind in our faces, half an hour of reading the Summit underpass graffiti, then south with the sun warm on our backs. All that summer we rode for free; for freedom.

Oh, there were moments. I took one pretty good fall, spent a couple of weeks with very little skin left on my arms, legs, and the left side of my face—told my folks I'd wiped out on my bike. They bought it, fussed a little. No big deal. Liz missed a few times (lacking in dexterity, in my opinion) and I either made the trip alone or jumped. When I left her behind on the gravel bank I got confused. First I'd feel superior, then bored, then guilty. The next summer she didn't miss as often and whenever she *did* I didn't go on without her.

It's funny, but we never talked very much. We didn't need to. We both loved the trains, the risk, the rush. We loved the wind in our faces, the feeling of flying. We could spend hours lying on the ground staring up at the sky and not saying a word. Liz came to my house a few times and my mother was polite to her, the way she was to the cleaning lady or to my guitar teacher, because he had long hair and smelled like marijuana. At least that's what I heard her tell my father when she thought I wasn't listening. Liz didn't seem to notice the politeness, but I noticed when I went to her house that her mother was very *impolite* to me, and somehow it felt exactly the same as my mother *being* polite, so I got the message. *(She pauses)* I was twelve, not stupid.

At the Summit underpass, we discovered a loose brick that could be worked all the way out with a little twist and pull. The gap made an ideal hiding place and Liz and I had our first serious discussion. What should we conceal there? Liz's mom smoked Kools and she figured she could pilfer a pack without getting caught. I got a couple of books of matches from the café where my sister was a waitress and we added a pack of Dentyne (just in case anyone decided to smell our breath), and a red felt marker for making political statements. It just seemed right to add this new dimension to our rebellion, and we took turns attempting to blow smoke rings—unsuccessfully—and adding to the Summit underpass graffiti.

There was snow in the air on our last trip before I turned thirteen and we made a pact to come back together on the first nice Saturday in the spring. To seal the deal, we restocked our hidey-hole with a fresh pack of Kools, gum, and matches. We put our initials and the date on the brick with a new green marker, added it to the cache, and then pushed the brick neatly back into place.

(Jen pauses, as she reaches for the next reminiscence, and her growing maturity shows in her voice and body language)

It was the spring when we were thirteen that a few other kids tried it. Liz had been bragging. It felt wrong somehow, like no one else should do it. If she took other people to the Summit underpass, would she also show them our hiding place? I couldn't help but wonder. We still didn't talk much, so I didn't ask her. Then Luther fell and everyone just kind of left us to it. I didn't care. I just loved the trains, the wind, the underpass, even the sunburn and mosquito bites. I didn't even care about the stolen cigarettes anymore. Liz smoked them alone, quiet, trying her hand at creative profanity with a bright blue marker.

It was a hot, humid summer day, when July is unforgiving and even a soft landing jump makes your sunburn sing. I rode alone when Liz didn't show. I lay on my back in a Summit Township field near the underpass and chewed on a blade of grass; tempted a garter snake to curl up around my wrist; admired the clouds. *(Jen frowns, as she begins to admit that things are not the same as they used to be)* I didn't like the underpass anymore. It was smoky and dirty, and the graffiti had gotten stupid. I wondered where Liz was and then realized that I wasn't really sure I cared. I rode the trains for myself. But I rode because she'd dared me in the first place...and it was still the coolest thing I'd ever done.

I heard the whistle and raced back across the tracks to grab the southbound train home. A creeping doubt was nagging at me and drove me from the train straight to Liz's door. I was going to have it out with her. Were we friends or not?

(Jen begins to move again as she takes the audience through the scene change)

She was sitting on the steps of the sagging front porch. When she saw me she got up and darted inside. The sound of a flat handed slap and a shrieked oath sent her scuttling out again backwards.

"Hey," I said, uncertain now that I was there just exactly why I was there and what I'd even come to say.

"Hey." She answered without turning.

The porch door flew open so hard that the lower hinge popped and the wood cracked. Liz's mother shoved her so that she fell back down the steps to the weedy, littered yard. I moved just fast enough to grab her shoulders and pillow her head before she hit the ground.

"You stupid little bitch!" the woman screamed at me. "Get out of my yard before I call the cops!"

I looked down at Liz's battered face. Her left eye was swollen bigger than my whole fist, her lip split in two places, and there were bruises from her hairline to chin. I couldn't speak.

"You want to kill yourself, you go head, girlie! But you leave my goddamn daughter alone, do you hear me?"

I could feel Liz quaking but I still couldn't move; couldn't speak.

"Are you deaf or just stupid?" she screamed. "Get off my property now!"

(Quietly)

"Liz?" I looked down at her—there were red spidery veins running through the white of her right eye.

"Just get the hell out of here," she ordered me as she pulled herself up. Her t-shirt hiked up in the back and I could see striped bruises across her tailbone.

(Jen pauses, emotionally, and moves
a few steps away from the scene)

I don't remember getting up or turning away. I don't remember running, but I was suddenly running with all my strength—straight to the tracks. It was nearly sunset and there was a train going south. I grabbed a rung, swung myself up, and held on. I leaned back as far as I could and let the wind dry my face. This was *my* ride! Only this time, I had no idea where I would jump.

PENNANT PENNANCE

A Dramatic Reading

1 Female - Kelsey

KELSEY: "Go girls! Bring it on home now!" He shouts beside me, thumping his big working man's hands together, painfully loud and close. I glance to my right, but he doesn't look at me. His eyes are on the field but a muscle is twitching in his jaw and I know he's thinking that I should be out there. *I'm* thinking that I should be out there.

"Thataway, Emily! Good slide!"

"One more!'

"No pitcher! No pitcher!"

Why can't I drown out their voices? Why can't I join them? What am I even doing here, sitting on these hard metal bleachers that are pinching my thighs? Why do I feel the sun burning my skin sitting here—I never even notice it when I'm out on the field?

I want to say, "I'm sorry, Daddy. Please forgive me." But I don't. I look down at the field. Coach is pacing along the first base line and he looks at the stands—right at me. Even from this far away I can see his jaw tighten and his eyes grow cold. I know that it isn't anger or hatred that I see. It's disappointment, which is so much worse. And I want to say, "I'm so sorry, Coach Molina. I'd take it back if I could. I'd do anything." But he looks back at the first pitch to the next batter and I don't say a word. I'm too far away anyhow, and it's been too long. I've waited too long.

The bat cracks and the high foul sails over the stands and into the parking lot behind us. All eyes turn my way. In my head I know that they're following the flight of the ball. But in my heart they're all staring at me. They're all thinking: *There she is. That's the girl who broke into the coach's office. There's the girl who blew her shot at a softball scholarship to St. Mary's her senior year.* Of course, most of them aren't really looking at me at all. Most of them don't even know me. We're 180 miles from home in the Section 6 final game. One more run and we're going to state. *They're* going to state, I'm not. Dad feels their eyes too, though. Beside me, I feel him stiffen.

**(Kelsey steps away from the present as she
relives the horrible mistake she has made)**

All I had wanted was to have some fun. But I didn't want to tell the truth, so there we were. I didn't want to do it. Mr. Molina never did anything to me, but I was afraid that if I didn't go through with it, I would look like a crybaby geek in front of Jake. If Nikki hadn't asked me to say who I wanted to have kiss me right in front of him, I never would have taken the stupid dare. She knew I liked Jake, just like I knew my dad didn't like him, or Nikki, or Nikki's boyfriend, Eddie.

Eddie and Jake swore that the school alarm system only activated with movement in the hallways and common areas, and that the office windows weren't wired. I was so afraid that they were wrong. They hid down in the bushes and I was the one doing a Spiderman along the wall and window ledge. If I couldn't have fit through that little window Coach leaves cracked it would have been all over anyway. I hoped I wouldn't fit, but I did.

"Hurry up!" Nikki hissed at me from below.

"Shut up!" I whispered back. "I'm doing the best I can."

I heard them laughing down there. The sweat had my hands so slick that I couldn't get a decent grip on the inside of the window frame and my lip stung where I'd been scissoring it between my teeth, but I couldn't seem to let up on it.

There was enough light from the street lamps for me to see into the glass-fronted bookcase where he keeps his autographed baseball collection.

"Grab a good one." That's all they had said. I reached into the cabinet and closed my fingers around one at random. I squinted at it in the darkness. Mickey Mantle. "Damn good one." I whispered. I turned for the window but my elbow hit something on his cluttered desk and there was a crash. I froze for a second and then raced for the window. They weren't laughing anymore, I noticed.

I went down a heck of a lot quicker than I had gone up, I'll tell you that much, and we all ran like crazy back to Eddie's garage where we'd been playing truth or dare and sneaking cigarettes from the carton of Camels his dad kept hidden in his tool box.

Inside with the door shut and the fluorescents shining, it all seemed pretty cool. Jake was impressed, I could tell. When I told them about it I pumped it up a bit, you know, kind of added to the drama a bit. The more I talked, the better it got, and Jake kept sitting closer and closer to me with his leg pressed tight against mine.

It was just a prank, I thought. Just a harmless little truth or dare. Jake noticed me, the cool kids accepted me, and I'd return the ball the next day. Oh yeah, I told myself all kinds of good lies. Only it wasn't harmless. And the *cool* kids turned on me, bragging around about the escapade and within a day I was busted. Coach and the school didn't charge me legally—but they suspended me for a week from school and for the rest of the season from the team. Coach didn't say a word. That's what hurt the most. He took the ball I handed to him and looked at it—never at me. He squeezed it and his face got tight, like he sucked his lips right back into his face so that there was just this hard straight line. He nodded as Principal Jax handed down his ruling but he never said a word. He still hasn't. My dad sat there beside me—mirroring Coach's expression and nodding. During the week I sat at home I got the letter from St. Mary's—withdrawing their scholarship offer. No explanation. Just…*After reconsideration for admission and scholarships…*"

(Kelsey forcibly pulls herself out of the difficult
memory and returns to the present)

The winning run is on third now. Emily. My best friend from fourth grade until stupidity. Gretchen, our second best batter at .371 is at the plate. It's the most exciting moment in our high school careers and I'm seventy yards away from the plate; at least fifty from the mound; *my* mound; and out of uniform. Suddenly I can't draw a full breath and I hear a sound reminiscent of my dog begging for scraps. My eyes are burning and my blink reflex is on overdrive. His hand closes over mine and squeezes hard.

(Kelsey forces her voice out and around the
lump in her throat as tears fill her eyes)

"Daddy. Oh God, Daddy! I'm so sorry." As quickly as that his arms are around me in a bear hug like I haven't felt in years and he's stroking my hair and rocking me.

"Sshh…" is all I hear. "Sshh now, baby, sshh…"

I haven't seen him cry since my mom died four years ago, but he's crying now. Not making a scene or anything like I am. He's just holding me while I let it all out and people scoot a little farther away from us on the bleachers. He still loves me, I can feel it. I had wondered. Now I know. He'll love me if I go to State U or Community College, if I play softball or if I don't. I'm sick to my stomach but I'm feeling—feeling—something. I can do this. *(Kelsey struggles with it, but gets her emotions back under shaky control)* My dad loves me. I can do this.

I hear the inimitable sound of a dead-on hit; aluminum on leather; feel the vibrations of a hundred people jumping to their feet on the metal bleachers, and hear the roar which tells me that Gretchen connected and Emily scored. I don't actually witness the win firsthand, but I feel it in every muscle of my body and I know what I have to do. He knows too, because he releases me, looks into my eyes, and nods. He turns back to the field and applauds with the rest, as I make my way toward the plate where my teammates are all gathered, celebrating, hugging, screaming.

My heart is pounding, the sound so loud in my ears that the cheering is distorted and unreal. *(Kelsey moves cautiously closer to the audience)* I walk as if in a vacuum toward the circle that I am no longer a part of, and my eyes focus on Emily, praying that I'll see forgiveness in her eyes and that I can find the strength to finally apologize to Coach.

Some of the girls see me coming, I know. *(She continues to move carefully, hesitantly to a nervous pause)* They nudge others who nudge others and I'm choking again, holding my breath. Emily and Gretchen are embracing in the middle of the huddle. I can tell when Gretchen notices me and says something I can't hear. *(Kelsey takes one more step)* Emily turns and her eyes lock on mine. I can't read her. *(Kesley takes one more step)* I stop. She hesitates. The next thing I know she catapults into my arms and is hugging me and jumping and crying all at the same time. How can this feel so good and hurt so much all at once?

"You shoulda been here," she whispers in my ear.

"I know. God, Em. I miss you. I'm sorry. I'm so sorry."

"I know," she hugs me tighter.

I know she means it, I can feel it, and it's so damn humbling I can't believe it. I'm reeling in all of this already when I blink to clear my eyes and see him over her shoulder. Coach Molina. His expression makes me freeze. It's like the day I returned the baseball all over again. His expression is hard and unreadable. But I avoided looking into his eyes then and was too scared then to let him see that I was scared. I wouldn't break contact with him now.

Maroon and gray uniforms separate around us and Emily draws back, but keeps her arm around my waist protectively, still sniffling. The air around me seems charged with expectation and everyone is watching, waiting. I owe my whole team, and I know that. But I have one more real apology to make and this one is the hardest for me. How can I expect the man who'd made me a good enough ball player to deserve scholarship offers understand that I had stolen from him and violated his trust just to impress a guy who wasn't worth it a few hours later? How?

I'm still wondering, still looking into those gray somber eyes, when I see the thin line of his mouth relax, the gray glitters a little, and his shoulders drop as he opens his arms for me. *For me.* Willingly I step into his embrace and whisper my plea as the crowd erupts once more. *(Kelsey pauses, closing her eyes in both pain and relief for a moment)* Coach Molina presses his stat book into my stomach and says, "I'll be needing a manager at State. It's getting to be too much for the old man."

Then he turns and walks away toward the cheering crowd, and I look down at the book. Emily puts her arm around me again and several of my teammates pat my back or shoulder as they pass. I won't be playing, I know, and I haven't really redeemed myself. Not completely. But I look at Coach's back disappearing into the crowd and hold the book tightly to my gut and know that at least I'm on the right road.

SWEET DREAMS

A Dramatic Reading

1 Female - Lara

LARA is speaking, conversing with her son.

"Why don't you go out on dates?"

"What are you talking about?"

"You know, dates. Why don't you?"

"Is dating the latest hot topic among eight year olds, or is this just personal concern for you old mom's social life?"

Mitchell giggles and gives me a gap-toothed smile before gobbling another forkful of macaroni and cheese. Personally I hope it's the end of the discussion. It's not.

"On T.V., grown up people always go out on dates."

"Oh they do, do they? I guess you and I must be watching different shows."

"It's true, Mom. They go to places for dinner and they dance and stuff. They get all dressed up, you know, Mom."

"Okay, Mitch," I say, deciding it's time to try a different tack. "I'll admit that in some shows there are people who date, but not on all shows and not all people. Besides, this is real life and not everyone dates."

His blue eyed glance drops to his plate where yellow cheese sauce has all but obscured the masked face of Batman, then focuses on me again.

"But why aren't *you* dating?"

"What's the sudden interest in my love life anyway? Why do you care if I'm dating or not, honey? *(Lara's voice gets progressively louder and more intense through these lines)* Maybe you don't see it but I'm completely happy with my life just the way it is, and dating isn't all fun and games, Mr. Nosey. Relationships are full of problems and some of them can't be solved in thirty minutes like they are on television." *(She deliberately stops herself, working for calm and control)* I hear my own voice – louder and more annoyed than I intend—and I take a deep breath. I shouldn't be speaking to Mitchell like this.

"I'm sorry, Mitch." I reach across the tiny dinette table that I had rescued from an early demise at the county dump, and cover his small sticky hand with mine. "But you, of all people, should understand. I know you're only eight, but you know things that a little boy shouldn't have to know…and you've seen things that a little boy shouldn't have to see."

Mitch looks like he's going to cry and I can't take it. Our crying days are past. I reach out to him and he leaves his place in favor of snuggling on my lap. He doesn't do that often these days. I stroke his blond head and kiss it softly. He smells of White Rain, cheese, and chalk—no man's cologne could ever be sweeter. The silence soothes and comforts as the light from outside fades from orange to purple to silver to black, and still we sit.

"Do you every miss him?" he asks.

"No." I find that I am unable to lie to him. *(Gently, kindly)* "No, Mitchell. I don't miss him. But if you do, it's okay you know."

For the first time since climbing onto my lap, he pulls away from my shoulder and looks directly into my eyes. I see telltale brightness, but he isn't crying. We *don't* cry.

His earnest voice trembles not in the least with his answer. "I hate him."

(Lara pauses, her expression is one that struggles between pain, and resolve to move forward. She steps away from center stage as time passes)

Dishes are done. Stories are read. Kisses are exchanged and prayers are said by the one of us who still believes. Soft light is filtering through the half open bedroom door, cutting the shadows across Mitchell's bed where I tuck the covers snugly around his chin.

"Mom?"

"What honey?"

"I love you."

"I love you too." I wait for him to go on, sensing that there is more. He just plays with the edge of his blanket, forming fuzzy fluff balls in his fingers. His forehead is wrinkled with concentration and he is biting his lower lip. Sweet quiet seconds pass.

"I just thought that maybe you would want to like somebody now."

"Now? I don't understand. What do you mean, *now?*"

"I mean that it would be good for you to like somebody now that he's really gone."

"Mitchell, he's been gone for more than two years."

"That's not what I mean, Mom."

I wait for him to go on but he doesn't. He's embarrassed for some reason. He seems younger suddenly, but his eyes appear infinitely aged and wise as he contemplates sharing his secret with me. Without taking my eyes from his, I sink to my knees beside his bed so he will know that I'm listening. "Honey, you can tell me. You can always tell me anything. What do you mean that he's gone?"

"He's gone from my dreams. I haven't had any nightmares about him for a long, long time. It's like he's really, finally gone. It's like I'm not afraid to come home from school anymore, or go to sleep anymore. I'm even starting to forget what he looked like, Mom. I'm starting to forget to always be scared and careful. You know, Mom?"

His voice has taken on a pleading quality, desperate for me to understand—to affirm his feelings, and to confirm his safety.

"You're absolutely right, honey. He is gone. He's gone from our lives and now he's gone from your dreams too. He can't hurt us anymore."

(Lara pauses, struggling to keep her emotions under control as she slowly moves back to center stage)

Funny…that lie wasn't so hard to tell, I think as I crawl between the icy sheets. Maybe Mitchell's nightmares are truly over now. If they are, I might just be grateful enough to regain some faith. But not likely.

As darkness closes around me I feel the accustomed struggle begin. *(For the first time, we see the depth of Lara's fear, and her expression of it should be sufficient to make the audience share in that vulnerability)* It's a struggle to stay awake when my body and mind are exhausted. It's a struggle to escape the voice that's calling; the hands that are reaching. And for tonight, it's a struggle to own what my son has finally found—the right to sleep without dreams, and the peace that cannot exist with fear.

IWONDER@AOL.COM

A Dramatic Reading

1 Male – Paul

PAUL: I met her at a reception following my presentation at the travel show. She liked my speech she said. She liked my smile. Our homes made a future get-together plausible she said. She gave me her email address – then she smiled back at me over her shoulder.

(Typing)
SUBJECT: Remember me?
DATE: January 16
FROM: iwonder@aol.com
TO: csanders@travelstar.aol.com

Hello Christine. Remember me? Paul? We met Friday. I've been thinking about what you said and I agree. Drinks at Cianni's on Saturday at 7:00? If you still like me at 8:00, I'll buy you dinner. What do you say?

Paul.

She said yes. What a night! Christine was more than beautiful. She was intelligent, sweet, funny, sexy – I was completely and unequivocally captivated.

(typing)
SUBJECT: WOW!
DATE: January 20
FROM: iwonder@aol.com
TO: csanders@travelstar.aol.com

Christine – that's all I can say – Wow! We parted only moments ago and I'm afraid I find myself compelled to tell you how wildly my head is spinning. I must confess that I am actually giddy with excitement. And prior to this precise moment in time, I can honestly say that I have never used the word "giddy" in my life! Counting the moments until I can gaze into those beautiful brown eyes again—

Paul.

I got her return message Sunday morning and my heart felt like it expanded to the point it might burst. *She* was feeling like *I* was feeling. Now don't get me wrong. I've had girlfriends. At least ten or eleven since I was a teenager. Three of them pretty serious. But those were several years ago, I knew in my heart that none of them was my soul mate. I had *never* felt this way about anyone before. Two dates later, I told her so.

(typing)
SUBJECT: You're the One
DATE: January 28
FROM: iwonder@aol.com
TO: csanders@travelstar.aol.com

Christine, my darling Christine. Oh, how I adore you. Please tell me that I didn't frighten you this evening by expressing my love for you so early in the springtime of our relationship. You are everything I have ever dreamed of in a woman, a friend, and a lover. I don't know what I did to deserve the advent of this joy in my heretofore colorless life. I realize now that I have lived as a blank canvas – stretched in the unyielding frame of boundaries I've placed upon myself. But suddenly, someone has touched me, with brush strokes so soft, and hues so subtle, that I am transformed. I have been alone for so long, Christine, that I have come to think of myself as a solitary soul in a world which moves past me two-by-two. But now, I cannot imagine a future without you by my side. I love you, Christine. And before I met you I loved the dream of you. Thank God you have come true.

Love, Paul.

It was a month of pure heaven. I could see our future clearly: a spring wedding, a house in the country that we would spend the summer fixing up…kids…right away! Two or three, maybe even four. I could see it all. Lord – how I loved her – and I made certain that she knew it.

Then things started to change. Sometimes she was "too busy" to go out, or even to see me; or "too tired to talk" when I called. That's all right though. It's not like I'm the needy type. A little space is a good thing. As long as I knew she was *mine*.

Then she said that we were moving a little too fast. Too fast?! I couldn't be-lieve it! She said she really thought we should slow down. "Slow down?!" I said, "Oh, this is just great. *You* want to slow down – and *I* was about to ask you to marry me!" Then she got angry. Can you believe that? *She* got angry at *me!!* She said that I was pushing her. She said that telling her I was going to propose right when she said she needed me to slow down was unfair and manipulative. *Me!* Unfair and manipulative? And then she left. Just walked right out.

(typing)
SUBJECT: Why?
DATE: February 27
FROM: iwonder@aol.com
TO: csanders@travelstar.aol.com

Christine, I love you. I can't help that. I love you so much that I ache in-side. Your withdrawal feels as cruel as the knife's edge of betrayal. Don't do this to me, Christine. Don't do this to *us*. We have the opportunity to rise above this shallow world. Our love can do that. It is an elevating force and I fear that I have attained a height from which a fall may prove to be irrevocably damaging.

(He steps away from the keyboard and begins to pace)

There was more. I poured my broken heart out – line after line after line – but she threw it all back in my face. She accused me of using my vocabulary as a weapon. "Emotional blackmail," she called it. I told her that I was trying to express myself eloquently—in the manner she *deserved*. But she said that I had crossed the line between "eloquent" and "pretentious." *Pretentious…me!?*

(becoming increasingly agitated)

Then she told me that her friends agreed that I sounded desperate and controlling. Her friends. *Her friends?!* How the hell do her *friends* know how *I* sound?! And that's when she told me that she had forwarded some of my messages—*my personal messages*—to her friends! To get their advice, *she* says—to humiliate me, *I* say! *You conniving bitch….*

(works to calm himself and resumes typing)
SUBJECT: Forgive me
DATE: March 1
FROM: iwonder@aol.com
TO: csanders@travelstar.aol.com

Christine – I am so sorry. Please forgive me, darling? I was wrong to push. Take all the time you need, please. Just don't shut me out completely. I need you so badly. I…
"Incoming message"…Oh my God, it's her…

(reading the screen)

Paul, you need help and I'm not the one who can do that for you. I can't be with you. You've pushed too far and there's no going back from that. Please—leave me alone. I'm truly sorry if I've hurt you, but please, Paul—just leave me alone!

(he wanders from the keyboard numbly at first then with growing anger)

Leave her alone? Leave her alone, she says. Only she *isn't* alone. She's with her friends – laughing at the lovesick sucker she's been stringing along. They all do it, you know. It's like a game to them. It's how they get their kicks: breaking hearts, shattering dreams. They're all alike. And *she* calls *me desperate, controlling, pretentious? She* wants to end it.....

(he opens a drawer and removes a handgun and magazine – stares at them)

Ok. Let's end it.

(he slaps the magazine into place, clicks the safety and stares again at the gun as a deranged smile replaces his devastation – and looks out to the crowd)

I'm coming, baby.

THE STATEMENT

A Dramatic Reading

1 to 2 Males / Staged 1 to 2 Males with courtroom extras
(Judge's lines may be used as a teaser, leading to Victor's Monologue)

JUDGE: The defendant will please rise. Victor Volture, you have been found guilty by a jury of your peers of the crimes of rape, criminal harassment, and violation of a restraining order. You have been sentenced to 25 years to be served at a facility to be determined by the court. While you refused to take the stand in your own defense, the court has been made aware that you would like to make a statement prior to beginning your sentence. I see that there are media representatives present—and I caution you, and the gallery—disruptions of the proceedings will not be tolerated. Mr. Volture, you may proceed.

VICTOR: Statement. Yes. I have a statement. I have a few, actually. First: a Public Defender? Ha! That is the quintessential oxymoron. No one person defends the public! Such a thought is inconceivable and anyone who thinks otherwise is as imprudent as the very man who thought of the absurd notion *(he laughs)*. The man whose expenditure is too great for his income is afforded NO defense whatsoever. Am I to defend myself in a court system built upon such a travesty? How? *(He sneers)* And what more travesties have you heaped upon me in your jury selection? A jury of my peers? THESE? Preposterous! To think that I would have relations with such filth would be laughable if there were ANY taint of humor in this air. Plumbers and cab drivers—I would NEVER sink so low as to even acknowledge the existence of these "people," and I use the term loosely. My peers!! To say that I am disconcerted would be an understatement.

I have been accused of criminal harassment, violating a restraining order, and the most ridiculous crime of all—the crime of rape. How is it rape when she wanted me?! I picked up on all of her little gestures. Every morning at 7:30, I would walk in and she would give me that inviting look—so bright and friendly. She KNEW she spoke to me with her eyes. Urging me. It was a look of lust and desire. I could tell! Don't you think I could tell?! She didn't just WANT me—she NEEDED me. I recognized all the signs: her full, painted lips tilting upward slowly as she asked me how I wanted my coffee, it was as if she were tempting me— daring me even—to take here right there. I am a respectable man—and I fought the urges brought upon me by her advances because I wanted to wait for our love to be true and enduring. But no—she wasn't used to such subtlety. When she handed me my coffee her fingers deliberately grazed mine. Still, I resisted, and you convict me. ME?! She wouldn't allow me to resist! She started wearing more provocative clothing, showing off her soft smooth skin *(he pauses with an evil smile).*

The day I knew her need for me pushed her over the edge was a troublesome day. I arrived at the shop at the usual time – anticipating the look of her soft warm face—but she wasn't there! Her obsession with me must have driven her insane. I tried not to jump to conclusions. Maybe she was in the back—so I waited. I waited for five hours and 23 minutes until she walked in—with a man. An abomination. As Robert Frost said, "You've got to love what is lovable and hate what is hateable and it takes brains to know the difference." Still I am a man of intellect and I knew that she was testing me, teasing me. That's when I knew that it was time. I wanted to surprise her, I wanted her to feel wanted the way I knew she wanted me.

You—you so-called "peers" cannot begin to understand what I felt! You only heard what you wanted to hear! The truth is that I was only giving her what she'd been asking me for all along. How can you accuse me of something so terrible when I didn't even provoke it? No good bastards! I went to her house. I knew where she lived. You see, I had followed her home a time or two—because I was looking out for HER!! I hoped that she would drop something—any small thing that I could pick up and return. Ah, now that would have been the perfect icebreaker. Her neighborhood was an invitation to criminals—so I'd watch and wait, to be certain she was safe. Oh, how I do ramble on— None of this is important. No. That night – the night I went to her house, I was going to surprise her. I went to open the door but it was locked. *(He smiles)* She was toying with me—testing me yet again. On the second floor, I could see a window open to the evening air—and it was plain that she wanted me to climb up to that window. What other reason could there be? She wasn't home yet, which gave me the opportunity to set the scene. I'm a man of romance; of a chivalrous nature. I searched her pantry and refrigerator, I set the table with her china and candlesticks—the finest restaurant in the city could not have been more beautifully appointed for our evening. I waited. Her face when she entered was—apprehensive—another test, to be certain. And yet another when she turned—as if to flee, but I was prepared for that— it's all a part of the game, you see. I caught her easily and sought only to end the months of longing and torment for her—and I kissed her. ONLY kissed her! But she—wouldn't—kiss—back. After all this time the selfish bitch *(he fights for self-control as he glares at her across the courtroom – and regaining his composure, laughs and looks at her with desire)*—Ah, well, Nathanial Hawthorne once said that Selfishness is one of the qualities apt to inspire love. *(He laughs again—then turns angrily to the judge)*

Can you see the fault in your accusations? I was just doing what she wanted! I only used the force she begged for when she so strenuously resisted. I only struck her head one time—ONLY ONE!! And only then when she screamed—because that's the way she wanted it. And YOU *(pointing at the judge)*—stand here in judgment of me? And YOU *(gesturing expansively toward the jury)*—find ME guilty?! What do you know of love? What do any of you know of what a woman who used her charms to tempt and tease needs when she finally wears down the resistance of the only man who truly understood her? You've sat here in judgment, listening to lies and have only now heard the truth of the case—and I can see on your faces that you are too dull of wit to even comprehend the truth of my story—so do your damndest. Lock me up for being honest. Lock me up for showing her the love she wanted. *(Sarcastically)*

I'm ready, your honor. *(He jerks his hands behind his back as though being cuffed roughly and takes a couple of small steps before turning back to the girl)*

By the way—I'm sorry if I hurt you. *(He freezes with an evil and knowing smile)*.

A CHANGE OF HEART

A Dramatic Reading

1 Female, 2 Females, or 1 Female and 1 Male

Characters: Mary Ellen Tucker
Reporter

Opening scene may be filmed and projected during blackout or performed live before change of scene to talk show setting.

TUCKER: The whites must reclaim this country! We must stand together against the hordes of human refuse that invade our coasts and borders daily! We must rise up and squelch the spirit of inferior races who are destroying the very fiber of America's existence! Are the parasites in *your* neighborhood? Are they in *your* workplace? Are they in *your* school? Are they shopping in *your* stores? Now is the time to reclaim our inheritance! Cast out the undesirables—*whatever* it takes! *(Freeze)*

REPORTER: Mrs. Tucker, after watching this recording of your own heart-rending appeal to other Klan members, other white suprema-cists—other bigots—do you honestly expect this audience to believe your claim that you've changed *so* much, that you are now an advocate of Civil Rights; defending the same people you previously dubbed "infe-rior parasites?"

TUCKER: I believe that my lifestyle now is evidence of my claim. I be-lieve that if your audience will hear me out, they will appreciate my trans-formation...my change of heart, if you will. Let me begin by saying that the tape you just showed sickens me. It sickens me to watch it, and to remember saying and feeling those things. And the fact that the tape was made at a KKK rally *seven years* ago does nothing to alleviate my shame.

REPORTER: Is it not true that during the period from March of 1982 through November of 1991, you were not only a member of the Klan, but that you held a position of some authority?

TUCKER: Yes, that is true. It isn't so much that I had the authority myself, but I had the trust of the Grand Wizard. I wrote his speeches.

REPORTER: Is it not also true that you had an active role in violence against people of minority races, and that there were incidents in which that violence led to deaths?

TUCKER: NO! That is not true! *(she struggles with her emotions – until her voice breaks free again)* Oh, God—maybe—maybe I was involved. Not overtly. I can only tell you how it was for me. My parents were Klan. I was reared that way. I was brought up to believe in *one* truth: white superiority. I lived daily with hatred and fear of other races. I joined the Klan when I was twelve—but, in essence, I had always belonged. I was *born* to it. I became a youth leader. It wasn't long before I discovered that I was a gifted writer, and a dynamic speaker—I had the power through my words to make people believe! To make them cry! To incite them to violence and fury! Yes! Oh dear God, yes—I was responsible for violence and probably for deaths—and I'm sorry. I'm so, so sorry.

REPORTER: So, your belief, all of your life, until just "recently" was in all the Klan stands for. So, what happened? To what do you attribute this miraculous transformation?

TUCKER: My daughter, Alyssa, who is nine, became friends with a black girl, named Tess, in our neighborhood. I forbade the friendship. I did everything I could to squelch it. But it continued. Alyssa began questioning my convictions constantly, and I grew angrier, and more afraid. I'm mortified now to remember the names I called Tess and her parents... how hateful I was to them. Alyssa despised me. She ran away, in the dark, in the pouring rain, off through the fields on the outskirts of town. She stumbled and fell into an abandoned mine shaft that no one even knew was there. When I discovered her missing, I was certain that she had gone to Tess's house again and I was infuriated. I ran to their home and... *(she breaks down)*

I deserved no sympathy, no understanding. Believe me, I cringe when I remember my words that night. But these people...they acted as if they heard nothing except that Alyssa was missing. They were jacketed in seconds, him calling the neighbors for help, her gathering flashlights, first-aid supplies, and a blanket. Within minutes there were a dozen people or more in their yard—all of them black. All of them knowing who I was...*what* I was, and all of them reaching out to pull *me* into their protective circle and to help me find Alyssa.

It was hours later when someone heard her stifled cries coming from the mineshaft. Two men rigged up a rope pulley. They were lowering Tessa's father into the menacing hole—and just before he disappeared from sight—his eyes met mine and I found myself whispering a prayer for *his* safety...for *his* life, as well as Alyssa's. He called for help and the first-aid supplies. Another man, one with every reason to hate me was going down the rope into the mineshaft. My heart was frozen in fear during those horrible minutes—by that time someone had called for an ambulance and police—but before the paramedics could start down, three dirty faces appeared and a cry of exultation erupted from the crowd of searchers—which looking around me, I realized had swelled to nearly fifty people.

I rode with Alyssa in the ambulance—listening to the paramedics tell me that no doctor could have splinted her broken arm and leg any better than what her rescuers had done. It was a long night, and through it all, six newfound friends were *beside* me, supporting, comforting, praying...holding *my* hands. I couldn't take my eyes off of those hands clutching mine. Black against white; dark against light; goodness and mercy against ignorance and fear. Tears welled in my eyes and the colors faded into irrelevance. I sobbed then—held by arms I'd sought to destroy, and in those moments, I was cleansed.

I had professed—always—to be a Christian. But until that night I hadn't known what Christian charity really meant—what *humanity* meant! In that moment, I knew that there is and can only be one race. One people. When we can all believe that…that we are all part of the human race, and that the color of our skin is immaterial in the eyes of God—then maybe the fighting and bigotry will cease.

Blackout and Freeze
During the blackout – the reporter moves to new set.
The spotlight picks him/her up.

REPORTER: *(bitterly)* Will they? What you have just seen is a tape of Mary Ellen Tucker's appearance on this very stage just one week ago. *(with some force)* Today, Mary Ellen Tucker is dead. Burned to death in her own home along with her daughter Alyssa; a swastika painted on the charred ruins.

(clearly, sympathetic to Mary Ellen Tucker) A transformed woman who has paid the ultimate price for that transformation. Not everyone, apparently, appreciated her "change of heart."

EMILY'S SONNET

A Dramatic Reading

1 Female - Sherry

SHERRY: Say you come from a dysfunctional family; an environment of alcohol or drug abuse; poverty; illiteracy; or domestic violence—and you'll find a sympathetic ear and shoulder to lean on at nearly every turn, right? But who is there to listen to you if you're normal—exceptional even? Who hears the child, the overachiever, who cries only when she's alone? The answer is simple: no one.

Emily Garrett had everything. From my earliest memories I was envious of her. Not that I have it so bad—I don't really. In fact, I have it pretty good. I realize that now. Emily and I grew up in the same neighborhood and we hung out with pretty much the same kids from preschool through this year. It's funny, looking back on it—but considering all the time we spent together, I didn't know Emily. *Really* know her, I mean. Of course, I knew all the superficial stuff—but I didn't know who Emily actually was, the person inside that perfect girl we all *thought* we knew. Maybe we were too busy envying her to really try—or maybe she just didn't want us to get too close.

Emily had a perfect family, in my eyes. Her dad was drop-dead gorgeous and absolutely too fine to look like a dad. He ran a successful sporting goods store and gave private tennis and golf lessons. Her mother was a buyer for Macys and was, undoubtedly, the classiest, most beautiful woman I had ever seen. But what I liked most about her parents is that they always seemed happy. They were nice to all of us kids, and really supportive of everything their own kids did. They never missed a basketball game, play, or concert. They'd be in the front row, cheering or beaming with pride.

Her older brother was a college football player and the local heartbreak king. Her younger brother was a little sweetheart who doted on everything Emily did. None of them could want for a thing. Their house and yard were like something from the cover of *Better Homes and Gardens*—beautiful cars, beautiful clothes, and vacations to places that the rest of us could only dream about.

The most amazing thing though, was Emily herself. People tell me that I'm pretty, but next to Emily I always felt like a dandelion growing next to a rose bush. Emily was so beautiful—with long, dark auburn hair and deep brown eyes—sparkly and dark. She had a ready smile that revealed perfect teeth, flawless patrician features, and a lithe, athletic figure. And she didn't just *look* athletic, she *was* athletic. She had the kind of natural ability that made coaches drool, crowds "ahh," and the rest of us mere mortals turn green with envy. Add to that natural ability that she worked herself like a dog, practicing, honing her skills to a fine peak. She was an incredible sight to watch on the basketball court—and at least three colleges had taken notice of her, even though she was only a junior.

Emily excelled in more than athletics. She was at the top of our class academically, she was musically talented, and stole the show from the lead actors when she took the stage in our last drama club production.

I keep wondering now, why I didn't see anything wrong with Emily. But all I can remember is that she seemed to do everything with ease and confidence. Emily never complained—n*ever!* A lot of us have puzzled over it trying to recall a time when we heard Emily even express some small displeasure. The thing is—she was a great listener. I feel guilty now as I realize that she knew much more about me than I ever tried to get to know about her. She seemed charmed—blessed. And frankly, I always felt just a little bit sorry for myself. My parents divorced when I was ten. I guess I've really clung to my hurt and bitterness over it all—and I leaned on Emily. Teri's mother has M.S. and is pretty much an invalid now—and *she* leaned on Emily. Meghan's dad is an alcoholic and her family really struggles financially—and *she* leaned on Emily. Michelle has a really tough time in school and she would have flunked out of Chemistry last semester if it hadn't been for Emily. We *all* leaned on *her.*

But what about Emily? Who did she lean on? I guess we all figured that she had it all together and didn't need to, *(pause)* I know better now.

For the last three weeks, Mrs. Riley, our English Lit teacher, had been teaching us about sonnets. We'd been analyzing content, counting out the metric pattern and rhyme scheme—and getting pretty much bored out of our minds. Then Mrs. Riley assigned us a project: to write our own sonnets. We had a long weekend to work on them, and they were due on Tuesday morning.

I guess Tuesday morning should have tipped us off somewhat… it was the first time any of us remembered that Emily didn't have an assignment prepared to turn in on time. She told us that she just couldn't manage to write a sonnet. We understood, really—ours were all terrible.

We had a game that night. Our last regular season game before playoffs, and we were undefeated going in. We won easily. Emily scored 26 points, came up with 21 rebounds, 14 assists, and had only 1 foul. She was carried around on our shoulders, she laughed, cheered, showered, and changed with the rest of us. She waved goodbye, ran into that beautiful house, into her private bathroom…and opened up the veins in both of her wrists with an Exacto knife.

I don't know if we'll ever understand. But at least we learned something on Wednesday morning when Mrs. Riley discovered Emily's notebook on her desk. It seems that Emily not only wrote her assigned sonnet…she wrote 36 of them…all eloquent and beautifully written in perfect iambic pentameter. And all filled with the pain of a beautiful 17-year old girl who felt so driven to succeed, so pressured to be the best, that she was overwhelmed and ready to implode. Through her sonnets, we came to know an Emily we'd never known before. We came to know a scared, depressed, and lonely girl who kept all her emotions bottled up until she just couldn't handle it anymore.

She had seemed so perfect to me. Anything she wanted she could do. Ironically, she's attained something now that many people strive years for and never achieve...her last, most poignant sonnet is being published, and in reading it, I feel how deep her pain was, and I pray that's she's found peace from the agony she expressed in these 14 lines.

Dear God, each day I live is hell to face,
The more I have to stand, the pain is worse.
My lungs ache from the furor of the pace
I run to keep ahead of Satan's curse.
The debt I owe to God and owe to man
Just climbs. I claw and scrape my way through grime;
Once a purity of whitened, smooth sand,
Now a home to all of the earth's sad slime.
Don't count on anyone to ease the load,
Just look behind the mirror – salvations shelf.
Don't blame yourself, it never really showed –
There's no one who could save me from myself.
Blood pours forth to greet the friend I made;
I welcome now the sanctum of the blade.

BABY FAT

A Humorous Monologue

1 Male - Doug

DOUG: It was January first—too long after midnight to cash in on the New Year's baby loot—and too soon after noon NOT to disrupt my enjoyment of the Bowl games. Margie was a trooper though, saving her really big contractions for commercials and instant replays.

Finally, little Dougie was born. Actually, he *WASN'T* so little—ten pounds eight ounces to be exact. Of course MY only thought was: Thank God, I'm a *MAN!* Margie's first response to being told Dougie's weight was that that was ten pounds eight ounces down—59 pounds two ounces to go. I bestowed a fatherly kiss on Dougie's spongy bald head and sent him off with a nurse, listening to Margie mumbling as she drifted off to sleep—reminding me once again that she'd been eating for two all these months. "Yeah, right." I thought. *"TWO SMALL COUNTRIES!!"* Then, having missed the Rose Bowl—why aren't there TV's in the delivery room anyway? – I took one of Margie's valiums and floated away. I dreamed of my perfect baby boy—a tiny replica of yours truly.

I awoke to his tiny squirming form being placed in my arms by a nurse. I pulled back the blankets for a better look. *HOLY COW!!* I guess Margie wasn't the only one the birth had been rough on! Dougie's head was cone-shaped and his face was sort of squashed looking. And those EARS!! I couldn't decide if they looked more like Mickey Mouse or Mr. Spock!! Obviously some sort of deformity on Margie's side of the family.

Two days later, Doctor Gordon pronounced Margie fit to go home—but admonished her to lose 60 pounds.

"60?!?!?!" Margie screamed! *"I only weigh 59 pounds and two ounces more than I did nine months ago, buster!!"*

Obviously the insensitive clods had NO clue how to deal with women. So I took over... *It's okay, sweetie, he didn't mean to imply that it was YOUR fault that you gained all that weight...* "

"*My fault?!*" she shrieked, shattering a mirror, "I*t's YOUR fault, you moron!!!*"

This accusation was punctuated with a finger poked into my chest—the bruise is still there!

She backed off when she saw that I had brought her a dozen red roses and outfits for both her and Dougie to wear home. But AP-PARENTLY—you can't squeeze back into size eight jeans directly from size fourteen maternity clothes. *I did not know this!* Nevertheless, I maintained my patience—I even dressed Dougie—before I picked the thorns out of my cheeks.

Knowing how Margie had missed shopping, and how she loves bargain hunting, I suggested we stop at a tent sale. Well, she burst into tears—accused ME of making jokes about her weight. I was crushed. Did I say she could *WEAR* a tent? I don't think so!! I tried to console her—said—"Aw honey, don't cry—there's just more of you to love!" But for some reason, that *REALLY* set her off. Anyway, I figured that this might be the wrong time to give her that gift certificate to Just Plus—so I took her shopping for the clothing of her choice. She was so frustrated within half an hour that she decided just to get some new pantyhose. We headed for her usual "No Nonsense" only to discover that somewhere along the way she'd slipped right off of their size chart—and on to the "Big Mama" chart. After she got done trashing the accessories department she picked up some "Big Mamas" and tossed them in the cart—carefully camouflaging them between a box of HoHos and 14 Hershey bars.

I tried to help, suggested various diets and exercise equipment I was willing to invest in. Through it all, she remained negative and de-pressed. She hated the treadmill, she smashed the new scale, and she bombarded me with cans of Slim Fast—knocking me down and then wrapping my necktie around the spokes of the stationary bike.

I was beginning to think that she actually didn't want my help. But, I decided to try one last idea. I suggested that Margie try the new aerobics studio down the street. It was worth a try. I offered to take her there and stay by her side. To my surprise, she agreed.

I was expecting bodacious babes in bright colored spandex. Imagine my surprise when we walked in on a group of grunting, sweating, bouncing, bovine beauties—straight out of Greek Mythology. They were being led by a human toothpick who looked as if she was possessed by the ghost of disco past! We ran for our lives—never looking back.

That's when Margie admitted that she was resigned to her new, unabridged body—and was all through fretting about her weight. Well, I told her that I love her just the way she is and said that I looked forward to her heat in the winter and shade in the summer. That's when I discovered that she really wasn't resigned—because she laid into me with words I never even knew she knew.

But then I hit on the perfect plan! I knew how to get her mind off all that silly old weight gain. We're expecting our second baby next month.

SLEEP STUDY

Ingredients:
Several well-intentioned doctors
Prescription sleep aids
Over the counter sleep aids
A white noise machine
Approximately 1,000 relaxation techniques

Results: No sleep, interesting side effects from various prescription sleep aids. Most interesting side effect? Homicidal fantasies of epic proportions and a firm belief that the perfect crime is attainable and realistically within my grasp.

Conclusion: Time for new prescription sleep aids.

Poetry

Featuring an award-winning performance piece written by my brother,
John, when he was only seventeen. John was too young when he
left this world, but he left behind family and friends who loved
him—as well as an impressive body of creative work.
The publication of "Scarecrow" is long overdue.

HOME

There was no warmth
Because there was no warmth
there was no love
Because there was no love
there was no respect
Because there was no respect
there was no trust
Because there was no trust
there was no faith
Because there was no faith
there was no home
Because there was no home
there was no place to hang my hat,
and so I went without;
bareheaded into a world where
chaotic wind fingers combed my
locks into whatever disarray
they chose so I could go on
searching without distraction
for the warmth

TIME TO LEAVE

When you've actually contemplated murder
...it's time to leave
When you've researched fast-acting poisons,
water to voltage ratios,
and estimated the velocity of a three story nose dive
and are pretty sure you could pull any of them off on a good night
...it's time to leave
When you've had one too many bruises,
have lost another friend...or tooth,
and you have no cheek left to turn
but the butcher's knife on the kitchen counter is looking mighty fine
...pack your bags, girl
Oh yeah...he may deserve it,
but you deserve better
...it's time to leave

SCARECROW

By John Allen Parker (1957-1987)

Yonder stands the Scarecrow, out in the field where the wind blows cold
and nothing stays for very long
We're burning it tonight
that's 'cause, well, the crows are back
and besides, no one ever paid it any mind
exceptin' Cecy.

See, Cecy's man got killed
and after that...she was kind of tetched
used to stand out there all night and sing to that old Scarecrow.

We finally had to lock her up.
Anyhow, we're burning it tonight.

—⟋⟍—

Well, it's almost night, and they'll be comin' fer me
well, let 'em come, I say
let 'em burn me.
Nothin' matters now that Cecy's gone.
Besides...
the Crows are back.
They always come back...
Tearin' me...teasin' me...
laughin' at God and makin' fun of Cecy!
Ah, poor Cecy.
The Crows say she'll never be back

that they tied her up and hauled her off in the back of the pick-up truck.
She could never have fought them off all alone, ya know, and I ain't
much help, bein' made of rags and old straw…

When I was first made and
stuck out here in this God-awful field
she was there…
her and the other kids
all crowded around my feet.
I liked them little kids
but they got tired of me, I guess
and didn't come to play after a while…
'ceptin' Cecy.
Cecy came a lot to see me.
Guess the kids got tired of her too.
She used to play games with me;
strange and wonderful games, where she was a fairy princess
all dressed in lace and jewels
and I was her knight…
Ah, we had us some adventures, me and Cecy…and the Crows didn't say
nothin'—
they was scared of me in those days…

Here they come again,
divin' at my head and swearing at me.
Foul birds!
I never done nothin' to 'em
and it's on account of them I'm bein' burned.
They flew to the farm house and bothered the old man
but they flew away when he showed 'em his gun.
Still, he ain't happy with me a'tall,
and after what's happened with Cecy and all
he ain't likely to let me go on like this.

Ya see, Cecy never really grew up
like the rest of the kids did.
She was always kinda dreamy and, aw, you know—gentle,
and she'd come out here and sing t' me…
real pretty songs they was
and she'd tell me things too…
things that hurt her too much to tell anyone else.

There was this boy,
And he hurt her real bad.
He took my Cecy's purity, and he told all the other boys…
that hurt her real bad.
She'd come out here and cry on my feet, sobbin' her poor little heart
out
and I just kept hangin' up here and couldn't do nothin'
…ah, I felt so helpless in those days.

It was about that time that the Crows came back.
They made fun o' my little princess
and I'd've killed 'em all if I could just have
freed myself.
But they was still wary of me
and kept clear of my arms…
But Cecy, she started comin' less and less—and the Crows, more and
more.
She'd go fer weeks without talkin' to me
or even lookin' this way.
Guess she finally grew up.

Then, one day, I was sleepin'
With the Crows settin' on me, pullin' at my straw
'cause they had found out what I was made of,
and up come Cecy

and brushed 'em off me
just like she'd never left me…
and God, she looked pretty!
Her eyes was shinin' and she was dancin'
all dreamy like when she was a kid,
and she looks up at me and says,
"Scarecrow, I'm a goin' now.
You've been a real pal, ya know?
But I'm a woman, fully grown, and it's time I was a-leavin'.
I've got myself a first-rate man, Scarecrow, and he wants to marry me,
so I'm gonna go with him now. Good-bye."
And she kissed me
Then she was gone
And I cried.
You wouldn't think I could cry, would ya?
Well, you don't know what it's like, either.
Hangin' up there on that cross, day after lonely day
wantin' to reach out to 'em
wantin' to tell 'em everythin' I know about the world…
the changin' of the seasons, and the secret laws the critters keep…
that folks just never see…and about…about
about bein' *made* and not *born.*
The Crows think that's real funny,
me not havin' an earthly father.
They make jokes about it and I can hear 'em laughin' in the dark.
Here they come again.
Can't they leave me alone, just fer a bit before I die?

It was the Crows that told me when Cecy come back.
They told me she was crazy.
I told them they was liars!
But they was right.
Cecy's mind was gone…

she was like a little kid, all dreamy and love-struck.
Ya see, Cecy's man, he got hisself killed in a huntin' accident
and her mind—it just snapped.
So she came back to me.
But no matter…things just couldn't be like before.
Cecy got so that she'd come out here at all hours o' the night,
just t' sing t' me.
But her songs was sad and lonely things, all about death and dyin' lovers,
and they made me cry inside.
But I never hurt as bad as Cecy hurt,
and one night, while she was out here singin'
some men came and took her away.
She fought 'em—she *did*, and I'd have helped her if I could've,
but I was up here and she was down there and there was a lot of men
pullin' on her—
and she was screamin'
"Scarecrow! Oh Scarecrow! Why can't our love be real?
Why can't it be all?"
But I couldn't answer 'cause there was other people there.

And that night—I dreamed!
I dreamed that in the field, there was this big, fancy dress ball,
like the kind that Cecy used to sing about.
All the critters was there, and that harvest moon hung in the sky like a
big ol' lantern,
all yellow and warm.
All the critters was havin' a high ol' time!
The wolf was dancin' with the deer and the snake with the toad!
But the grandest of all was me and Cecy.
She was like me, all clumsy and crazy-quilt!
And I took her in my arms and we danced.
But as we danced, it was like the moon was growin' and all the critters
was gettin'

closer to Cecy and me—but she was so pretty, and it felt so good to move that we just danced on...but the moon kept growin' and growin' 'til it was pushin' against the clouds and all the stars, and the critters kept gettin' closer and closer, and I finally just had to talk, and I says, "Cecy," I says, "I...I..." but the dream broke off and fell, and blew away like a piece of dry sod in the wind...
And there was nothin' but the Crows,
cacklin' at the Sun and mocking me in my pain...
but that's the last I ever saw o' Cecy,
and I'm glad of it.
That's how I want to be rememberin' her when they burn me.

So, it's night now
and they're comin' fer me.
I can see their torch lights down by the old garden wall.
Well, let 'em burn me.
The sooner the better, or not at all.
Come on, farmer.
Come on, death.

We burned the Scarecrow last night. Just dropped a match, and poof! It was all over.
But it seems kind of strange when I think about it.
All of us standin' out there in that field at twilight, just to burn it...
and the little one says, that as it burned, she heard...
a whimper...

ABOUT THE AUTHOR

Jennifer Parker earned a bachelor's degree in English Education, with an emphasis in writing, from Bemidji State University. She went on to obtain a master's degree from Grand Canyon University and currently works as a high school English teacher, theater, and speech coach. She also works on a part time basis as a radio announcer.

Parker comes from a family of writers, including her son, Perrie Cronin-Cole, author of a non-fiction scientific study; her sister, Mary Jo Parker-Jepson, who has published two non-fiction history books, and her brother John Allen Parker, whose work appears in The Insanity Cookbook. Her brother, Stephen Parker, a graphic design artist, created the cover art for the book while Parker's son, Ian Cole, an editor, technical and screenwriter, did the editing. Her mother, a book reviewer, and her father, "the best storyteller ever," were also instrumental in its creation.

24906961R00085

Made in the USA
Charleston, SC
10 December 2013